Published by Author Level Up LLC.

Version 4.0

Cover design by MiblArt.

Editing by BZ Hercules and Audrey Weinbrecht.

Special thanks to Zachary M. Chisenga (consultant on rodent biology), Ken and Jodeen Bristow, Teresa Roberts, and Jonah White (consultants on the city of Chicago), and Toni Hyman and Alexandria Muro (general beta readers).

Very special thanks to the following patrons who support the author on Patreon: Stephen Frans, Jon Howard, Michael Guishard, Beth Jackson, Megan Mong, Lynda Washington, and Etta Welk.

This is life's sorrow:
That one can be happy only where two are;
And that our hearts are drawn to stars
Which want us not.

— EDGAR LEE MASTERS, SPOON
RIVER

CHAPTER ONE

CYRUS GRANT TUMBLED BLINDLY through the storm sewer, fighting for his life. Somewhere beneath the streets of Chicago, his animal form agitated round and round like a balled-up sock in a washing machine.

He couldn't see anything. Not since he had shifted into a rat. The pitch blackness of the storm drain combined with a rat's legally blind vision made sure of that. The drain was too small for him to shift back into human form. If he did, he'd block the flow of water, break his back, and drown. Hell of a way to go. So he had to ride this death river, and he was certain it would be the last thing he ever did.

He broke the surface of the cold, foamy water violently and oxygen rushed into his lungs.

Liquid sewage effervesced around him. His body twisted as the current yanked him under. His whiskers rubbed against something that sent a constellation of smells to his brain that he knew without knowing. A messy soup of garbage: a condom—old, sagging, and reeking of latex—a hand sanitizer bottle with traces of aloe gel, a disintegrating banana peel, shards of glass, an empty pack of cigarettes, and the soggy remnants of a Chicago deep-dish pizza crust.

And, of course, human shit. A whole crescendo of it underscoring the darkened landscape. Creamy, wet, stinking shit. It was more than he wanted to smell and taste right now, but his rat brain never stopped discerning scents, even on the verge of death.

He flipped wildly around, gasping. His tail, as if it had a mind of its own, sliced through the sludge like a rudder, always righting him just before the current dragged him under again. But even his tail was losing strength now. He slammed against the wall. His high-pitched squeaks were lost in the chaos.

Nothing could survive down here. Not even a rat.

He was fighting to live because he had crossed the members of his mischief and they'd attacked him. He fled into the sewers, and now here he was, ready to die any minute.

An alcove in the wall spilled a column of filth onto him. The intense cold knocked the wind out of him. The jet of water buoyed him up and then pushed him down, down, down into even deeper darkness than he thought was possible.

Just as his head broke the surface again, the water's deafening roar relented.

Though he couldn't see it, his whiskers swept back-and-forth across the water, confirming that something was ahead. Whatever it was, it smelled different…like air.

Fresh air.

With newfound energy, he pedaled like he'd never pedaled before. The current jerked him under one final time before he rocketed out of the water, into the night, into the stars.

Time must've slowed down. With his terrible eyesight, he gazed at the blurry face of a crescent moon ringed with storm clouds. Even in low definition, the sky was so beautiful, in a tragic sort of way, as if it were the last thing he might ever see.

Then time snapped back to normal and Cyrus crashed into the frigid Chicago River.

The river carried him solemnly, and he regarded the night sky, regaining his breath.

The roaring sewer current faded into a melody of cricket song, cars zipping over a nearby bridge, and the rumblings of a storm dancing somewhere over the suburbs.

The sky. The air. Instinct took over as his whiskers swept the water again, steering him toward a hazy gray line that blunted the side of the river. A shore.

If there was anything Cyrus learned since he had become a shifter, it was that shifting hurt. Bad. As his claws dug into sand and rock, his bones popped like old suction cups. His spine lengthened. He screamed as his rat hair burned away into wet, stinking skin. His incisors shrank into his jaws as if tiny humans inside his skull were reeling them in with pulleys.

The face of the moon, originally blurry, sharpened into high definition and full color, surrounded by stars. His eyes shook in their sockets. As he grew, the rocks scratched his knees, and his tail slapped sediment on his chest as it receded into nothingness.

Gasping, he lay on the rocks, his clothes covered in thick, disgusting excrement. He stared up at a graffiti-strewn, twinkling bridge that divided the navy sky into diagonal halves.

Just yesterday, he had been sleeping on his sister's couch, homeless and looking for a new job. Now he was a rat, running for his life on the shores of the Chicago River.

He was supposed to be playing video games or going on a date or sitting on a rooftop brooding over his ex-girlfriend instead of this. Anything but *this*.

Everything came rushing back to him. He had crossed his mischief, gotten into a rat fight with Zane, the self-proclaimed alpha, and Zane pushed him into the current as punishment.

If Zane found out he was alive, he'd come hunting for Cyrus to finish what he'd started.

Even though every bone in Cyrus's body ached, he had to keep moving. He couldn't stay here.

He pulled himself into a shamble toward a grassy clearing knotted with streetlights. Beyond that, a cluster of brick apartment buildings loomed beyond the trees. He had no idea where he was, but he couldn't have been far from downtown.

It was going to be a long night. He'd have to shift back into a rat at some point. If he didn't get hunted by his old friends, run over by a car, or attacked by a pack of wild rats, maybe he'd have a chance at staying alive.

His thoughts swam as he fell into the grass on his knees. Then he got a whiff of himself and vomited. The stench was unspeakable; normal to a rat but stomach-churning in his human form.

He had been turned into a rat. A fucking *rat*.

There was only one man who held the answers to his transformation and the possible cure. And with the mischief hunting him now, he wasn't long for this world…

He had to find Dr. Thurston.

CHAPTER TWO

Two Years Ago

It happened at dusk.

The evening sun, a red-hot burning disk wreathed in cirro-stratus clouds, sank into the horizon, casting the first night shadows across Dr. Atticus Thurston's office.

The doctor, engrossed in editing a scientific report that he'd been working on all day, raised his head and looked out his window on the 35th floor of the Alsatius Building. He'd lost track of time. The other researchers had gone home and their workstations were stacked with tidy messes of papers. Had they even said goodbye to him? Probably. The waning sunlight in the cavernous skyscraper valleys of downtown was always enough to remind *him* that it was time to go.

He'd marked all over the article with a pencil that he had worn to a nub but was using anyway because time was too precious to walk across his office to the pencil sharpener that his secretary had bolted to the wall for his convenience. Every minute counted when you faced a looming deadline.

He distinctly remembered that there was something he

should have been doing right now. He gazed out the window, trying to jog his memory, but he could only think about rat vibrissae, or whiskers. An albino rat inside a cage, moving them back-and-forth, standing up on its hind legs and sniffing, its whiskers having a bad hair day.

Then his thoughts jammed. He rubbed his temples. His hands were covered in streaks of graphite and eraser scraps. He wiped them on his khaki pants and tried to think, when he became aware of a soft rhythm.

The Newton's Cradle on his desk. The metal balls clicked against each other—separated, clicked, separated. His wife bought him this pendulum for his birthday. When he first unwrapped it, he pushed it aside in disgust, saying it was too clinical. This was the kind of thing you'd find in a psychiatrist's office, not a biologist's. But it added a manmade touch of coldness to a desk that was quite literally covered with rats —taxidermied albino rats pinned to aluminum rods, arms and legs stretched out like Superman's, with asymmetric, cotton-balled eyes that looked like pus. Their whiskers fanned in all directions. Brushing the back of his hand against the dead rats' vibrissae reminded him of poking oneself with a blade of grass.

And then he remembered what he was supposed to be doing.

Sighing, he picked up the green phone on his desk and cradled the receiver between his head and shoulder as he dialed.

"It's me," he said in a soft voice. "I'm on the way."

"I was wondering if the rats had eaten you," his wife Eva said, cold at first. But then she brightened. "Please tell me you're almost done with this busy season."

"As soon as the university pays me, you'll see so much of me, you'll wish I was back in the office," he said.

"We'll see if getting enough of you is possible," she said.

"I like where this is going," he said, laughing and leaning back. "Tell me more."

On the other end of the phone, a baby cried in the background, and then Atticus felt guilty, thinking of his daughter, probably sitting in a highchair for dinner, food all over her face, strands of blonde hair over her eyes.

Eva deserved a nomination for sainthood. Wouldn't it have been nice to clock in at seven and be home by five again? Have weekends like a regular person, with Chinese takeout, foot massages on the couch, and maybe even a Cubs game? Why did his daughter crying remind him of normality?

He was married to an amazing woman with infinite patience. At some point, they'd talked about Eva going back to school for culinary arts. She'd missed her calling in life. When that time came, he'd be spending a lot less time doing overtime. No more deals with the city. Just time at home, chasing kids around, dreaming about his other kiddos here in the lab...

"Atticus?"

"I'm here," he said quickly, shoving some papers into a leather bag. "I'll be walking out the door in five. I know you've got to be starving. What can I pick up on the way home?"

"I wouldn't stop," Eva said.

"But it's Friday. I'll grab dinner at Mariano's at least. Something from the salad bar."

"But haven't you seen the protesters?"

"Protesters?"

"You know, the only people more disgusted by your life's work than me," she said. Atticus detected a smirk. "It's on the news. Animal people, apparently."

"Here we go again."

"Be careful, Atty. I know they mean well and all, but—"

"It's fine, babe," he said, grinning. "If things go south, I can always run to the sewers. The rats know me."

"Why does part of me think you're actually serious?"

"I'm one hundred percent joking. I've got a heavy leather bag and an umbrella I can use if I need a weapon. I'll go old lady on anyone who tries to start trouble."

He told her he loved her and hung up. Then irritation set in as he grabbed his pea coat and Chicago Cubs baseball cap off a coat rack near the office door.

The animal people again. It was always the goddamned animal people.

The city of Chicago had a rat problem. For years, it was voted the "rattiest city in the United States" by pest control professions, beating even New York City. At night, thousands of Norway rats—*rattus norvegicus*—emerged from sewers, burrows in the ground, floorboards, and other godforsaken places to feast on garbage.

No part of the city was spared from the brown invaders; infestations were reported downtown, on the south side, and even in suburbs to the north. This year, the rat problem was particularly bad. Rats bit babies as they slept, sensing sweetness on their breath from dried formula. They raided faculty lounges in elementary schools and even roamed the halls during the day. They terrorized back alleys and parking lots; walking to your car in some areas was like re-enacting a scene from a B-list horror movie. The rodents were even known to ride the L from time to time, getting on and off with late-night passengers.

People had had enough. There were protests at apartment complexes, at City Hall, and community centers. The city renewed its "War on Rats" and established a new task force.

People wanted to live in peace. No more Hail Marys before you opened a dumpster. No more smell of rat urine every time you entered an old basement. No more lifting a toilet seat and hoping that you wouldn't have a floating, wet surprise of the *rattus norvegicus* variety staring at you. No scratching in the walls at night, or waking up in the morning and finding the unpleasant and odorific surprise of rat droppings in your kitchen.

Not even public safety initiatives could solve the problem. On every alley telephone pole, city workers stuck yellow posters of an evil rat in crosshairs, saying that the area was being treated. Yet bait stations sat unexplored, turquoise rodenticides and wood snap traps inside untouched. The people who bought cats hoping for a quick solution were sorely disappointed, especially when the rats started attacking the cats.

A beacon of hope among the unwelcome, prolific invaders? A nationally-renowned lab in downtown Chicago partnered with universities in Miami and London, and a trade association of pest control professionals and consultants. A lab flush with investment money that, ironically, studied albino rats to solve the city's rat problem. Though these lab rats were far removed genetically from their wild cousins, they shared many commonalities, namely, social behavior and biology.

Atticus Thurston wrote his dissertation in the basement of an abandoned factory, surrounded by Norway rats. Fierce, brown Norways that weighed two pounds each with banana-yellow incisors. The kind of rats that would make even a gang member jump on the hood of their car and shriek like a little girl.

The novel part of his dissertation was that he released a pack of albinos into the wild to mingle. What happened was frightening: the territorial fights, the fear, the elevated stress levels in the lab rats as they learned how to survive in an environment that not even their ancestors had experienced for hundreds of generations. But eventually, they discovered how to get along, and even thrive.

Thurston's papers set the scientific world on fire.

Now he worked as the lead biologist for Allied Labs, a

nondescript private research facility on the 35th floor of the Alsatius Building on State Street, right on the river, in the heart of downtown Chicago, in the heart of the Midwest United States, and in the heart of the rat wilderness. These days, he studied rats' vibrissae and their function in helping them explore. Understanding their navigation habits was key to assisting pest control professionals reduce the rat population, which seemed to multiply every year.

The vibrissae were also where his troubles started. During the height of the rat protests, the local news learned of Allied's work and asked to interview him.

He gave a tour of the lab. He had been so enamored with the fact that the whole world was watching him, that people finally cared about the one thing he had studied his entire professional life—rats.

He got carried away. He led a young, scarf-clad reporter into "the stacks," the area where the lab kept rats in tall shelves that opened and closed by rotating large metal wheels. He rolled out a seven-foot-tall tower full of rats. He grinned with delight as the reporter beheld dozens and dozens of frightened white rats. Their jewel-red eyes gleamed among steel and cedar shavings. Their hair—a common response among rodents when threatened—stood on end.

"They live like royalty," he said. "Wild Norways never have it this good."

After giving the reporter a play-by-play description of their routine and diet, Thurston made his fatal error. He pointed to a rat in the corner of one of the cages and said, "See anything missing with this fella?"

Of course, *he* knew what the problem was, but he wanted her to guess.

The cameras were still rolling. He was as buzzed as if he had had two glasses of wine.

"My study right now is with rat vibrissae," he said.

The woman stared at him. He might as well had squeaked rather than talked.

"Whiskers," he said quickly. "There's a lot of scientific evidence that suggests that they use their whiskers much like a blind person uses a walking stick. Rats would be legally blind, you see. But more fascinating is what happens if you clip a rat's vibrissae."

"You clipped its whiskers?" the reporter asked, incredulous.

"Just to see what the effects would be," he said. "Turns out it creates problems."

He then told her that he didn't like to do it, and that hurting rats didn't bring him any joy. The lab went out of its way to provide the rats with pain relief, something that had assuaged ethics concerns even among his peers at other labs. He cited an oft-used statistic in the scientific community that millions of lab rats gave their lives for medical purposes to improve our own, and that was never lost on Allied Labs. He just wanted to make a difference.

But the damage had already been done.

The story aired the next day. He and his wife viewed with elation. The story—a one-minute segment within a five-minute report, analyzed what Allied Labs was doing to curb the rat problem.

It did far more than instill confidence in the city's residents. It pissed them off. Royally.

Almost overnight, he received horrible voicemails from people and letters from all fifty states.

"How about we cut off your nose and see how you 'navigate'"?

"How does it feel to be a murderer?"

"You, sir, are a son of a bitch."

Thurston took the insults personally. He called the news station to ask for another interview, but the reporter didn't return his messages.

Ever since, he always believed he was misunderstood. Just like rats.

As he rode the elevator to the granite-walled lobby of the Alsatius Building, he caught a glimpse of a small crowd of protesters across the street carrying placards with his name on them.

Stop abusing rat babies!
Respect Mother Nature!
"Ratticus" Thurston sucks!

They chanted with their fists in the air. Not even the wintry Chicago wind deterred them.

They must've known his schedule. Maybe there was someone in the lab who told them. He was friendly with everyone, but his enthusiasm didn't always translate when it came to research. Was there a "rat" in the lab?

He thanked God that the protesters couldn't see him through the tinted windows of the lobby.

A black security guard with rectangular eyeglasses and a goatee squeezed from behind the front desk to meet him. The security guards in the building barely acknowledged his existence until the protests started. Then they never forgot his face and went out of their way to treat him with deference. Their butts were on the line if something went wrong.

"Ronnie, tell me good news," Atticus said.

"I had a killer ham sandwich today, and we didn't have any shoplifting in the stores on the first level," Ronnie said, "but as it pertains to *you*, Mr. Thurston, I don't have any good news."

"It's that bad?"

"We've got an officer out there right now," Ronnie said. "He's been there since three. Those folks are angry, but they're not causing any trouble. Let's hope it stays that way."

Thurston paused and looked through the revolving doors outside, where he could see the protesters walking in circles across the street, yelling his name. If he went out there now, it would be bad news.

"I'll call a car if you like," Ronnie said.

The lab paid for black car service if Thurston ever needed it. It struck him as excessive. Plus, he had an aversion to rich people services. He was just a lab researcher and the son of a secretary and sanitation worker. Riding around in fancy cars just wasn't in him.

"I'll save you a phone call," Thurston said. "How's the alley today?"

"You gotta be kidding me," Ronnie said.

"Unless the protesters thought about camping out at the loading bay, I'd say that's a pretty good escape route, wouldn't you?"

Ronnie sidled over to the front desk and glanced at the security cameras. He picked up the phone and had a brusque conversation with someone. After he hung up, he looked at Thurston over the tops of his glasses and said, "Suit yourself, but once you set foot out of that alley, I can't do a thing for you."

"I wouldn't dream of asking you to do more," Thurston said, waving.

A literal hop, skip, and jump off a loading bay later, Thurston landed in the darkened alley behind the Alsatius Building, among dumpsters and delivery trucks. The skyscraper rose in a dizzying, dazzling array of steel and wavy black reflective glass.

He skidded on a patch of ice but caught his balance and headed for a thread of light on the other end that would deposit him on the other side of the building. The alley was narrow and long, and it broke into an L halfway through. It should have been enough to bypass the crowds and give him a few hundred feet of cushion before ducking into the covered stairway that led up to the State/Lake L station.

A shadow darted in front of him, and he smiled.

Despite the fact that he was running away from people who hated his very existence, he was among friends now. Well, *he* considered them friends, but they would bite him and infect him with heaven knows what disease faster than he could blink. But if he had to pick between his enemies and wild rats, he'd choose the latter.

He could hear the protesters' chanting even now, though muffled. His name. How they cursed his name. All over a misunderstanding. Some part of him wanted to charge them, curse them out, and tell them how the news reporter took him out of context, and how an edited video was wrecking his reputation. But they wouldn't listen to him. There was no convincing someone who was convinced you were the son of Satan himself.

He rounded the bend in the alley and made his way toward the bustling street ahead. Pedestrians and cars passed by in a hurry on their way to somewhere important. He flipped the collar on his pea coat, pulled his Chicago Cubs baseball cap down to his eyebrows, and dug a hand into his pocket as he flowed onto the sidewalk.

He tasted skin and wool, felt the warm slam of someone else's body. Static electricity danced across his cheek. He recoiled. Then—a whack against his skull, his back arching in pain, his foot slipping up from underneath him as he crashed into a brick wall.

A woman lay dazed next to him. She was dressed in a brown puffy coat, a wool beanie, and tall leather boots. Her red hair fell over her face, and she groaned as she tried to figure out what had just happened.

Thurston wiped his head and straightened his cap, shaking away stars. He pulled himself up and extended a hand. "Are you okay? I didn't see you."

"That makes two of us."

The woman looked at him with green eyes and cheeks full of freckles. One tooth grew crooked in the top of her mouth. She smiled sheepishly as she took his hand. She was probably half his age—maybe early twenties.

For a few seconds, they stared at each other, and her eyes widened at the sight of his, like she was gazing deep within him. She scanned his face, and her jaw hung a little, and he noticed her maroon lipstick.

"I guess it was my fault," she said, wobbling as she took his hand. Her hand was warm and radiated furnace-like heat. The warmth suffused up Thurston's arm. Then she broke her gaze and laughed.

"Are you sure you're okay?" Thurston asked.

She smoothed out her coat and dismissed his question. She straightened her beanie.

She searched the sidewalk for something. Thurston spotted it a millisecond before she did—a white placard, face-down on the cement. Through the thin poster board, he made out the faint outline of his name.

A knot bloomed in his throat as someone called out.

"Hey, that's him! It's the rat man!"

CHAPTER THREE

PRESENT, One Day Before Hell Broke Loose

Cyrus didn't remember the order in which his sister ruined his sleep: curtains ripping open a hole of white-hot morning light, the aroma of Costa Rica blend coffee drifting into his nose, the cabinets slamming shut as if to spite him awake, or the rock-hard punch in the shoulder that said "Get up."

He jostled awake, one leg hanging off the couch. He was wrapped in a fleece blanket. An empty bag of cheesy puffs sat on his chest, staring at him like a bass in mid-feeding.

He wiped his face and startled at the sight of his sister, Becca—pony-tail, starry night bandanna, stud in her cheek, dragon tattoo on her shoulder, trademark camo tank top. She was frowning. Hard.

"Jesus, Bec. What's up with you?"

Becca grabbed the blanket and pulled, unraveling him off the couch and onto the floor. Frowning some more, she moved to the bay window in the living room of one-bedroom apartment and twisted the blinds open, flooding the room with sunlight that might as well have made Cyrus burn out of existence.

She sat at her reclaimed wood kitchen table next to a brick wall and nursed a hot coffee mug.

"Seriously, Bec, what the hell?" Cyrus asked.

When she didn't answer, he shot to his feet, staring daggers at her.

She gestured to his spot at the two-person table, where a steaming coffee mug and two slices of toast were waiting for him.

"Cy, sit with me."

Great. She was pulling the big sister card again by talking down to him. He folded his arms.

She pointed at the chair more forcefully this time.

After a moment of hesitation, he slid into it, arms still folded, suppressing a yawn.

Becca studied him for nearly a minute. She sipped her coffee, sighed, and said, "You. Need. To. Move. On. She doesn't love you anymore."

Each word was like a slap.

"Geez, how about a side of shade to butter my toast while you're at it?" he asked.

"I can't do this any longer," Becca said. "I let you stay here because I love you and I felt so bad for you after your breakup. But now, every day is like Groundhog Day. You sulk around through the shop, barely talking to my customers, and then you come up here and cry yourself to sleep with Jules's name on your lips."

Oh. So she wanted to fight now. Kick him while he was down. No one had any right to mention Jules. No one.

"Jules is my business," he said.

"Jules is someone else's business now," Becca said. "You're living in a weird alternate universe where every breakup song lyric is somehow true, like she's going to storm the building calling your name and begging you to come back."

"Okay, so I listened to a little too much Bee Gees last night," Cyrus said. "But what's the harm?"

"The harm is that you're living inside yourself," Becca said. "Which is to say you aren't living at all. And God, the fact that you even listen to the Bee Gees at all is creepy. We weren't even alive when they were big."

She set her coffee mug down and stared at him with tough brown eyes. "It's going to be okay. Life goes on, Cy. I love you, but you need to find somewhere else to live."

Cyrus's jaw hung open and he raised his palms in offense. "But I don't have any money."

"I'm paying you every day at the coffee shop," Becca said.

The $11-an-hour job at the coffee shop his sister owned was a godsend, but hardly enough to live on. He did some mental math and hung his head.

"It's only been two weeks since I've been here, and a month since we broke up," he said. "I'm still grieving."

"Jules is alive," Becca said. "That doesn't qualify as grieving."

"You're telling me you never had your heart broken?"

"More times than I want to count," Becca said, rising. "It's not like I want to make you homeless or anything. I'll give you a few weeks."

She opened a kitchen drawer, pulled out an envelope, and slid it across the table. "Here's a few hundred dollars. This is a loan, got it?"

Becca would rib him every week until he paid it back. He didn't know which was worse: accepting the money and enduring the pain or being broke. The former was probably better.

"Thanks, Bec," he said.

"Good. Now I get to tell you what you're going to do today."

"I don't have any plans," Cyrus said, shrugging. "It's my day off."

Becca smirked. "Day off! That's cute. Nope. Here's what you're going to do. You are going to go to the new Logan's Crossing shops that just opened. You are going to buy a nice shirt. Not a hoodie, and *not* a t-shirt. You're going to buy a button-down shirt, like the ones Dad used to wear. Do you remember what those look like?"

"Screw you."

"You're going to buy a shirt, brown shoes, and a nice pair of pants that don't have rips in them for a change. You're going to put those clothes on and wander around the storefronts like a lost puppy until you see a 'help wanted' sign. You're going to apply for a job and use me as a reference. Unfortunately for you, I'm the only one you've got."

She wasn't going to sit here and tell him what to do. Wasn't it his life?

"And one last thing. I wouldn't be upset if you cleaned the bathroom," she said, grinning.

"I might as well feed you bonbons while I'm at it," Cyrus said.

"That would be amazing, but you're broke and you're not spending my money on bonbons."

He slouched and took a bite of his toast. Becca was the only sister in the world who would damn near break his neck by pulling him off the couch to wake him up, destroy him verbally while he was half-asleep, give him money, and then feed him breakfast like nothing ever happened.

He felt guilty, like he was freeloading and taking advantage of her. He didn't know how to say anything that wasn't snarky, but maybe she was right. Getting out of her hair might do them both some good. They just kept snapping at each other lately. On the pissed-off scale of one to ten, Becca was a seven right now. Once she got to around eight, she left scorched earth in her wake.

"And you might want to call Mom too," Becca said. "She's worried sick about you."

"I'm not sick and I'm not dying," he said.

"Why don't you tell *her* that?" she said. "I'm tired of telling her you're fine."

She grabbed an apron off the hook near the front door and tied it around her waist. She primped her bandanna and said, "I gotta go back down. I left in the middle of a rush. When you come back, I can't wait to hear all about your new adulting adventures. Welcome to adulthood, kid. It's a bitch."

Cyrus shook his head as she slipped out of the apartment.

He finished the toast and then raided the fridge for milk and poured himself a gigantic bowl of Cheerios. He sat on the couch, surrounded by candy wrappers and empty potato chip bags, and he ate in peace while watching anime. At some point, he got a whiff of himself and thought maybe he ought to clean up.

Becca worked long hours at the coffee shop and bar. She had used part of Dad's life insurance settlement to start a business. It had always been her dream. For the first year or so, she almost didn't make it. But now the Wicked Cat Coffee & Brew was a popular and trendy coffee destination in the Logan Square neighborhood on the city's northwest side—a coffee shop by day and a bar at night. *Chicago Magazine* even put the Wicked Cat in its top ten coffee shops earlier this year, including an interview with Becca. His sister—tomboy Becca —was running a successful and renowned coffee shop and bar, hiring and firing like a pro, and slinging lattes and martinis with equal skill, all while doing what she did best—telling people what to do. He was proud of her. She had done something with her life.

Him? A college dropout in his senior year, which mortified his mom…a professor at the college. He was twenty-four years old, crashing on his sister's couch, and listening to love songs all day. At least, that's how it was now, after Jules broke up with him.

He opened the envelope that Becca gave him. It was full of loose twenties. Definitely looked like tip money.

Great. Becca was guilting him even more. A wave of tenderness washed over him. Maybe one day he'd be there for her like she was for him.

He dumped the leftover milk from his cereal into the sink and wiped crumbs off his face.

He'd do everything Becca told him to, but there was one thing he had to do first.

He had to see Jules.

CHAPTER FOUR

THE ALLEY behind Becca's apartment building was narrow, long enough for Cyrus to get a good run on his electric skateboard before rocketing out into the streets. He leaned forward and down, with the chicken wing-shaped remote control strapped to his wrist. He adjusted his black helmet, stickered all over with his favorite band logos and random stickers he collected over the years.

He caught a straight stretch and the board's motor hit full whine as he wove between cars whose drivers honked at him. He blew through a stop sign and hit his max speed as a sense of calm washed over him.

He'd had this board for several years, and it saved him an ungodly amount of money on public transit. Why take the train or bus when he could ride? It was a warm spring day in Chicago, the kind of day where people drove with their windows down, everyone wore sunglasses, and the sunlight reflected off every surface, even the sidewalks. Plus, Chicago was about as flat as a city could get, perfect for maintaining top speed on the board for a long time.

He adjusted his helmet and adjusted his sunglasses,

stealing a glance at his red high-top Converse sneakers just before he slowed to a stop at a red light at a busy intersection.

A black Tesla stopped next to him. He bet his board could beat it across the intersection.

With a quick press on the back of the board, he flipped it up into his hands and waited for the stoplight to change, hunched over a little. When the light changed, he threw his board down with a sly roll and jumped on.

The Tesla didn't stand a chance. He cheered, cut off two pedestrians with a sharp right turn, and swerved into a bike lane, accelerating to top speed again. As the coffee shops and office buildings and jewelry shops and banks and pizzerias and insurance agents and pharmacies blurred by, he started thinking again.

He passed by an old white bicycle locked to a street lamp, with someone's name stenciled on a sign attached to the bike's body. These ghost bikes were all over Chicago, reminding him of how dangerous it was to share the road with cars.

Yet he did his best thinking on the board. There was something about being a blind spot away from death or critical injury that made him think about his own life. About Jules.

She had drifted into his life like most people—by chance. A Latino heritage celebration on the northwest side in a lush, emerald-green park. He and his friends were waiting in line for a food truck that sold the tastiest tortas in town. He'd never had a torta before. He walked up to the ordering window and asked what it was. The cashier, a middle-aged Latino man, barely spoke English.

A voice next to him said, "It's a Mexican sandwich. Do you like chicken or beef?"

A petite, fair-skinned woman stood next to him. She wore a green blouse and maroon shorts. Eighties style. Curly brown hair in a bushy afro.

He was immediately smitten with her, but there was no way he was in her league, let alone the same planet.

She ordered for him in Spanish, and when the cashier handed him a steaming beef sandwich with a side of brown salsa and radishes, the woman smiled, winked, and said, "I'll take a commission, please."

He blushed and cracked a ridiculously corny joke. She laughed and walked away, leaving him staring after her for a while before the person in line behind him coughed politely to tell him to get out of the way.

Cyrus wasn't very good with the dating thing. *Of course* she was probably interested in him. He was too stupid to tell in real-time.

"You didn't talk to her?" his buddy had asked.

"She was just being friendly," Cyrus said, biting into the torta. "I was lost trying to read the Spanish on the menu."

"Bro, you are the most sheltered dude I have ever met in my entire life."

"Just because I went to private school doesn't mean I—"

Somehow his brain caught up, and he realized the missed opportunity. His buddy encouraged him, told him that he needed some love in his life. Even more appealing, his buddy told him that if any attempts at a date failed, he'd buy groceries for the next week. Being broke and desperate for a relationship, Cyrus worked up the courage to approach her.

What did he say? He didn't remember the exact words, but he asked her if she'd like to get ice cream sometime. It was the only thing he could think of as she looked into his eyes. But that was not how it came out, because she thought he was asking her to go for ice cream right then, in the middle of a festival that she was attending with her friends. Her face corkscrewed with confusion, and his awkward utterances didn't help. After another odd exchange, she said, "I'm not one hundred percent sure what you're trying to say, but if you're asking me on a date, okay."

And then it began. At Becca's advisement, he brought her flowers on the first date, which worked, but then he embarrassed himself royally by accidentally getting stuck in a revolving door with her at the restaurant he took her to. The door seemed big enough for two people, and he let her go first, slipping in after her. The next thing he knew, he was inadvertently grinding her, and her face was forced against the glass, making her look like a fish as she told him to get off her. The building security guard had to hit the emergency shutoff for the revolving door to bail them out…

Hell of a way to start a relationship, but she must've liked him enough to keep him around.

Four dates later, she kissed *him*. Four dates…He was too shy to make the first move.

He could still remember Becca slapping her forehead at his dopishness. "It took you that long to *get* kissed? I'm so embarrassed for you."

No initiative, she had said. He had many personal qualities; initiative wasn't one of them.

Yet he fell for Jules hard. Every day solidified his feelings: walking through Logan Square Park with her, talking about nothing at all; learning random Spanish words from her everywhere they went; riding on the L late at night after a movie with his arm around her, deep in conversation about philosophy and the weird and wacky ways of Chicago people. He loved how she'd smile with her eyes closed every time he told a terrible joke, and tap him on the nose with her finger just before she kissed him with all of her body.

Then he'd really fallen for her. One morning, after she'd slept over at his apartment, in silvery sunlight, in the afterglow of a long night of sex, he woke up alone. Jules had overslept and had to rush to work, but he didn't know it at the time. He called her ten times in a row and was a nervous wreck all day. He felt like an idiot when she told him the real reason she'd left. And yes, she'd been thinking about him all day. Nonstop.

From that moment, he could see his entire life with her; he had it all planned out. She was going to school to be a paralegal, and he would figure out what he wanted to do with his life at some point. They'd live in Evanston or Skokie, away from the city, in a nice little house with a postage stamp front yard. Maybe have a family. And they'd be happy.

Hadn't she wanted that?

A car horn tore him from his daydream as he blew through a red light. He flipped off the driver. Nobody ever paid attention to boarders.

He hung another left past an auto body shop and hopped onto the sidewalk, where he slowed to a stop.

Jules lived in a red brick apartment building. He remembered the pastel-colored walls that Jules loved—every room was a different color, straight out of the 80s. And the creaky futon they slept on. And the kitchen barely big enough for one person in which they constantly bumped each other while making dinner.

"Cyrus, you're a great guy," she had said on the day she ended it, on her front steps. "But I don't see a future with you."

"But I thought we were on the same page," he said, caught off-guard.

"I'm sorry, Cyrus. It's just that…we're moving too fast. I just need some space."

"Space? But we talked about moving in together—"

"I guess…I thought it would feel different, you know?" she had said, leaning against the wall on her porch.

"No, I don't know!" he had yelled.

She had tried to let him off gently. She spoke quietly, kept apologizing, and was overly polite. At one point, he started crying. Then he started yelling. Then she started crying, and the conversation turned into a shouting match. They both said things they didn't mean. His internal voice kept telling him that he was being an idiot, yet he couldn't stop the words from coming out of his mouth. He couldn't stop the pain in his heart, the pounding fear that no one would ever love him again. Like the whole world was expelling him from even the remotest possibility of love. Through his words, he had lashed out like a hurt animal. The breakup ended with Jules cursing him out and slamming her front door in his face.

He fell into a depression and got fired from his job at the anime shop for calling in sick too many times. His buddy who roomed with him took a job out of state and Cyrus couldn't afford to live in the apartment alone. Next thing he knew, he was on Becca's couch.

Jules never even gave him a reason. At least not one that made any sense. A six-month relationship, over in five minutes.

Their time together had been so tender and special…and yet he'd never met her parents. She never told him she loved him, even after he'd said it multiple times. He just told himself it would come, that her reply would come in due time. He told himself that one day she'd love him the same way he loved her. She'd catch up. And yet, deep in the bottom of his heart, he knew that she was drifting away from him, but he couldn't bring himself to accept that it could possibly be true.

A car playing loud *banda* music flew by, pulling Cyrus from that night and back into the present. He glanced wistfully at the apartment again—if things had gone better, maybe he'd've been living there with Jules right now.

He sighed. If Becca knew he was here, she'd probably kick his ass.

Yeah, he should've left. It was stupid to come here, but he had to. It was best if he left now that he had gotten the nostalgia out of his system.

He started to push off, when someone called him.

"Cyrus?"

Jules was behind him. She carried her trademark golden purse and wore a green sundress, the one he always liked. The afternoon light cast a halo-like glow in her afro. Big, black sunglasses covered her face. The very sight of her made his stomach lovesick.

"Uh, hey," he said hesitantly.

Now was his chance. He searched for the right arrangement of words, the right phrases to say to apologize and convince her to take him back. But all that came out was an unintelligible stutter.

Jules's face changed from confusion to anger. Her eyebrows slanted and she pursed her lips. "You need to leave."

"I was just passing by," he said, swallowing.

"I know that's not true," she said. "I told you: we're through. What part of that don't you understand?"

He wasn't going to give a snarky reply this time. He didn't know what he was going to say because before he could say it, a car door slammed and a tall Latino man jogged to catch up to Jules on the street. He wore an unbuttoned Hawaiian shirt with a white tank top underneath and looked like he bench-pressed cars for his workout routine. He even had a thin mustache. Cyrus hated him on sight.

"You Cyrus?" he asked.

"Let me guess," Cyrus said flatly. "New boyfriend."

"Your worst nightmare," the guy said. Jules held him back and said something in Spanish.

"Get out of here," he said.

Someone called across the street.

"Hey, Steve-O, you got trouble?"

Two brown guys in tank tops and jeans shorts climbed from a beater car.

Cyrus backed away.

"What's up, white boy?" one of the men asked.

"This is the guy running around here for the last few days bothering Jules," Steve-O said. "Now we finally get to talk to him."

The two men approached.

"Back the fuck off," Cyrus said.

"Or what?" one of them said.

"Everyone, stop," Jules said. "Cyrus, I'm so sorry this didn't work out, but it's over, okay? Please go away and leave me alone. Nothing's going to change."

"He can't take a hint, baby," Steve-O said.

Cyrus put up his fists and circled them around his face like he'd seen people do in movies. The two guys laughed. Then they dashed at him.

Cursing, he panicked and turned to run away. He didn't see another man who had snuck up behind him, fist already mid-arc toward his face.

CHAPTER FIVE

ATTICUS READ the crowd as they approached him. All young women, wearing winter jackets and carrying placards that could become murder weapons.

"How about you stop torturing rats and we'll stop chasing you?" someone asked.

He glanced down the street to the entrance of the Alsatius Building. A police officer sat in a squad car, facing the opposite direction.

The hair on his neck rose. Something told him to run, and he did, straight toward the stairs of the L station a block away.

Footsteps scudded on the sidewalk behind him.

"We're going to hold you accountable!" someone shouted.

Jesus. They were going to rip him apart. And that was if he was lucky.

Distance was on his side. He was bolting up the riveted stairs to the L station faster than he thought his feet would carry him. On the first landing, he paused and looked back. The protesters were just starting to climb. At the back of the group, the woman in the puffy coat followed them, wandering as if sleepwalking, her eyes locked on him, a stunned expression on her face.

What was the *matter* with her?

He took the stairs two at a time now, rocketing onto the train platform. At a turnstile, he fumbled in his coat for his transit card and tapped it on the terminal. It beeped red at him.

"Damn you!" he said, tapping again. The system beeped in acceptance, and he pushed his way through.

He glanced at the overhang display screens with transit times. Two minutes until the next arrival. In about 30 seconds, he'd be ripped to shreds.

He dashed for another set of stairs leading back down to the street. By now, some of the pursuers were hopping the turnstiles, pointing after him.

Where was a boy in blue when you needed him?

One of the protesters must've been a sprinter because she flew forward, arms blading the air, yelling after him.

"We have demands," she cried. "Listen to our demands and we'll go away!"

He reached the top of the stairs and started down, but he looked back at the crowd. He misjudged a step and, suddenly, the world was spinning madly around.

His shoulder hit the ground with a crack. He bounced, flipping on his side, smashing his nose, sliding down the stairs in a half-surf, half-roll.

It happened so fast, he could barely react except inhale as he slammed onto a landing and his body folded upon itself like a camping chair.

Voices, footsteps, train brakes, and car horns swirled together, distant now, like a reverie.

"Oh my God!"

"Learned his lesson the hard way. Damn."

"The train's coming. Come on, let's go."

Then screams. Were they screaming at him?

"Somebody get a medic!"

Shuffling feet. Train brakes squealing. A computerized voice announcing that the doors were opening on the left.

A warm hand touched his. A woman's face hovered over his.

The woman in the puffy coat. She was…smiling at him. Her face was full of color again.

"I was wrong about you," she said, her voice multiplying itself in his delirium. "But everything is going to be okay."

He found solace in her voice. Her face circled his, and she tilted her head, smiling so brightly that her eyes closed a little. If he didn't know any better, he would have sworn that his vision filled with heather and honeysuckle just before he blacked out.

He woke in a field. He lay, covered in dust and dirt, staring up at the twilight sky. Prairie grass wavered around him. A river roared in the distance. Golden evening hour rays eased across his face.

He blinked several times and sat up. Despite the twilight sky and in the ribbons of gold, orange, and brown that streaked the sky, there was no sun—not even a glimmer of moon or stars. Just endless shimmering yellow, and orange.

He rubbed his shoulder. He'd cracked it on the stairs, but there was almost no pain now—just ghost pangs that reminded him of his pursuers.

"Where am I?" he asked.

A woman was suddenly right next to him. Naked, with red hair pooling on the ground, grass and yellow flowers strewn throughout. She looked at him with emerald-green eyes.

"I told you everything was going to be okay," she said, taking his hand in hers. Her hand still burned like a furnace. "You wouldn't believe how many favors I had to call in to get you here."

He pushed her hand away. "What the hell's going on?"

"I healed you," she said.

He glanced around, taking in the endless countryside. The place seemed oddly familiar, and then he wondered if this was what Chicago looked like before Chicago was Chicago.

"You had us riled up," she said, stroking a finger across his cheek. "We don't take kindly to animal abuse."

"Who are you?"

"It's a long story," she said. "But you won't have to worry about us anymore. You're all right, Dr. Atticus Thurston." She emphasized the word doctor. "Maybe you aren't so bad, Mr. Rat Man. You showed me your inner love light. Now that I've seen it, I'll never let it go."

He should've pushed her away. He distinctly remembered that there was…somewhere he needed to be. Someone waiting for him. His stomach roiled, but her touch healed it, sending ripples of joy through him until his soul hummed.

"I just…" he said, straining through the joy, "I just want to thank you."

She pressed him into the grass and straddled him. She put a finger to his lips, leaned in close, and said, "Why don't we focus on healing the rest of you that's broken?"

He breathed her honeysuckle essence, let her put his hand on her face and trace an outline of her. He closed his eyes with pleasure as his world erupted with passion, bare skin, spinning fractals and flowers, and honeyed light.

He gasped awake into the L station, a dejected mess lying on the steps. People skipped down the stairs and around him.

He pulled himself against a railing, rubbing his shoulder.

He startled at the thought of the protesters, but a quick glance at the platform confirmed they were gone.

The last bits of twilight hung in the sky as swaths of navy overtook the Chicago skyline.

As he gathered his leather bag, stretched his perfectly healed body and caught the five forty-eight train, he thought of the woman in the meadows and still tasted her.

"There is something you can do for me," he remembered her saying as buildings flew past the train window. "But you really should go home first, Atty."

His stomach churned like the last time he'd had food poisoning.

The rest of the ride home and the walk through his neighborhood of wavering trees and old graystones was a blur. He moved on autopilot as he climbed the limestone steps to his apartment building, slid the key in the lock and crossed into the lobby, rode the elevator to his floor, and stumbled down the dark hallway to the green door at the end of the corridor.

His autopilot canceled when his key didn't fit in the lock.

He checked his key ring. It *was* the right key.

He rapped on the door, his stomach churning harder. He remembered that he'd forgotten to pick up dinner like he promised.

Footsteps padded to the door. There was a pause. The security chain jangled and his wife flung the door open.

She looked at him with confusion. She wore a blouse with a golden necklace. Her blonde hair was tied into a bun. She leaned against the doorway.

"Babe," he said. "I got attacked at the station."

Should he tell her about the woman? He would have to. But his stomach hurt too much and all he wanted to do was lie down.

"That's all you can say?" Eva asked.

"I don't...know what else to say," he said. "I've got to rest."

"Not here you won't," Eva said, her face twisting into a

rage. "You left me alone for a year and come back talking gibberish?"

Thurston's eyes widened. "I just spoke to you an hour ago."

A blonde-haired girl toddled across the living room, making grabby hands at him.

His daughter hadn't known how to walk. She could barely crawl just an hour ago!

"I don't know how else to say this," Eva said, "but we've moved on."

She moved slightly, revealing stacks of cardboard boxes in front of the bay window in the kitchen. The apartment was mostly empty.

"Eva," he said, "I don't know what's going on."

She hung her head. "Atticus, I can't do this anymore. The constant phone calls asking where you've been. The sleepless nights worrying sick about you. And—Bronwyn. Spending so much time without her father. It's just…I can't—"

"Eva, please. I just need to—"

"We'll talk tomorrow," she said. "But I can't talk to you tonight. I'm sorry, Atticus."

Tears welled in her eyes as she shut the door. The last sentence had hurt. She said his name with such coldness, as if she had never loved him.

Thurston stood in the hallway as if he had been struck in the chest with a hammer. Autopilot kicked in again as he stumbled down the hallway, the world teetering as he rode the elevator to the ground floor and stepped out the back service door into the alley. A streetlight flickered on.

He finally got to sit down—next to a dumpster overflowing with trash. Something shifted in one of the bags in response to him. A brown rat stood on the lip of the dumpster, chewing and staring at him. Then it disappeared into the trash.

Visions of Eva and the woman in the meadow swirled around his mind, becoming one.

He wept for everything that had been. His life, his wife, his rats, and many more things that he couldn't explain. But mostly, he wept for the woman of heather and honeysuckle who had loved him.

CHAPTER SIX

IN A FITTING ROOM MIRROR, Cyrus turned and inspected himself wearing a blue denim Oxford that he left untucked, a nice pair of khakis, and his brand-new swollen eye that he got for free.

It was tender to the touch. He pushed the red lump under his eye socket, hoping the swelling was better. A river of hurt exploded down his face. He let out a little cry, trying not to wince.

The bastards broke his sunglasses too, so he couldn't use those to hide his eye.

He raised a blue slushie cup to the swelling—the only first aid kit he could afford between Jules's apartment and this store.

He buttoned the sleeves and regarded his sorry state. At least the clothes were fine. His mother might have said he looked handsome if it weren't for the swollen eye.

He definitely wasn't going by Jules's anymore.

So Steve-O was the kind of guy she wanted. The masculine, alpha type.

Cyrus was a lot of things; alpha wasn't one of them.

Fine. Let her find out that those kinds of guys just wanted one thing, and they'd never care about her feelings.

Had *he* cared about her feelings? Visiting her just now? There wasn't any love in her eyes. Just annoyance. That was all he was to her now.

Stop thinking, Cyrus!

No more Jules today. He had to find a job.

He paid for the clothes in a rush, wearing them at checkout, which irked the cashier. He ignored the horrified look from her as she stared at his eye. Then he emerged into a lively block of storefronts on North Milwaukee Avenue and North Sacramento.

The building was newly constructed and controversial as hell, taking the place of a shady flea market that Cyrus and Becca were both glad to see go. As tacky as the old megamall was, with cheap socks, western wear, silver shops, and dollar stores that no one visited anyway, a lot of longtime residents didn't want the new complex of ornate brick, modern apartments, and retail spaces with sparkling glass fronts because it drove real estate prices up—a constant argument in Logan Square because of all the gentrification, like many areas in Chicago. Residents complained of the neighborhood losing its original charm. But politics always prevailed, and Logan's Crossing was built, and the swanky new lofts filled with tenants who were happy to pay the sky-high rent. Here it was, with the smell of hot food and coffee in the air, cars breezing by with windows down, and young people walking and laughing on the streets with pastel-colored shopping bags.

"Here goes nothing," he said, shifting his backpack's weight, staring at the long boulevard of shops ahead.

~

"Tell me about your experience with customer service," a store manager said, eyeing him in the middle of a customer rush. They were surrounded by candles. She grabbed a fat glass candle off a shelf. It had an image of a long pier stretching into an infinity of crystalline ocean waters.

"Tell me how you'd describe the scent to a customer."

He whiffed it and coughed. The cloyingly sweet aroma reminded him of his grandmother's perfume, and how a simple hug choked him with it. But he caught himself from being brutally honest.

"It smells like...fresh laundry?"

"Um, hello," she said wanly, tapping the oceanic image with a fingernail, "the candle should have given it away."

Cyrus chuckled nervously and rubbed the back of his head. "So when can I start?"

The woman crossed something off on her clipboard.

"You do realize that this is a *jewelry store*, don't you?"

As a store manager in an impeccably tailored gray suit stared him up and down, Cyrus gestured to his shirt.

"Right. I left my suit at home. And I totally understand that I look like I just got my ass kicked."

"Now that you mention it," the manager said, frowning.

"But that would make me the best jewelry salesperson you ever had," Cyrus said, tapping his temple. "Because I know what it means to lose something important. That's a transferable skill. I can channel this feeling when I'm protecting your jewelry, you know?"

The manager just walked away, leaving him with a goofy grin on his face that quickly faded.

"I know what this looks like," Cyrus said, standing next to a rack full of plus-sized bras as the assistant manager, a tall middle-aged woman, stared at him in disbelief. "But I just need a job. I swear I'm not a pervert."

She laughed him out of the store. Even after he left, she was still laughing.

~

"You're looking for a job? You need a doctor, buddy."

A Middle Eastern man at a burger and hotdog joint eyed him more with pity than seriousness. Glistening hot dogs circled on a rotisserie on the counter.

"You do realize that we keep late hours, right?"

"I thought this would be a nine-to-five gig."

"Strike two," the man said.

Cyrus slapped a five on the counter. "If you aren't going to give me a job, at least give me some food to eat."

~

He stopped for a break in the shade of an oak tree. Through the leaves, he glanced up at the sun and clouds. It was already four thirty. The light was starting to turn to the golden glow of evening. In any case, he could give Becca a report—a failing one.

He had walked into every shop that had a sign for help wanted. Even Target wouldn't take him.

Either jobs were for suckers or he was unemployable. The hiring managers couldn't stop staring at his injured eye.

There had to be someone at this place that would take him seriously. Wasn't there one person in this whole damn city with an ounce of sympathy?

Less than ten seconds after sitting down at a bench to eat his hotdog, he spilled mustard on his new shirt. He dabbed the stain with a napkin and cursed. Then he buried his head in his hands, saw that he had accidentally dropped his hotdog on the sidewalk, and he groaned.

Maybe it was a good night to listen to the Bee Gees again...

He touched the raw nerve near his eye again, and he suppressed a yelp. His slushie was lukewarm and useless now.

Something brushed against his leg. Under the bench, he spotted a blur of brown racing away before a pinkish tail slapped his foot.

Was that...a rat?

His brain caught up with his senses and he yelled, pushing away from the bench and jumping to his feet.

"Rat!"

No one heard him.

The brown rat had dragged his hotdog to a nearby tree circle and was nibbling on it.

"Why don't you eat my pride while you're at it?" Cyrus said.

Maybe it was his cue to go home.

Someone tapped him on the shoulder.

"You weren't hurt, were you?"

A wiry man in a checkered button-up shirt grabbed him by the shoulders. He had a patchy, grayish-black beard and rectangular glasses. "I'm terribly sorry."

"Sorry for what?" Cyrus asked.

The man knelt and made a clicking sound with his tongue. The rat with black eyes emerged from the tree square, stopping for a moment, and then running into the man's outstretched hand, still chewing. He scooped up the rat and brushed its hump with his knuckle.

"He may look wild, but he's a lab rat," the man said, stroking the rat's chocolate brown fur streaked with black. The rat's eyes boggled, almost bulged out of their sockets for a split second as it ground its teeth together.

"Are you nuts?" Cyrus asked. "You walk around with a pet rat?"

The man soothed the rat and held it eye-level with Cyrus. "I was just taking him out for fresh air. Usually, he sticks his head out of my bag from time to time. The smell of hotdogs must have gotten him excited."

Cyrus caught a rustic floral scent. The man wore a boutonnière pinned to his shirt pocket: a wreath of baby's breath circled with acorns.

"I'm glad you're all right, young man," the man said. "And sorry about the hotdog. But say—since I have you, could I borrow ten to fifteen minutes of your time?"

Cyrus was about to remark how he needed to get home.

"It's for a paid interview," the man said quickly. "It's the least I can do for scaring the bejesus out of you."

Cyrus started to speak again, but the man walked away and gestured to follow.

The man crossed out of the street and toward a shop inside an old masonry building that he hadn't noticed before. He passed under a red neon sign with the store title and stark letters: Whisker & Claw. A paper sign in the window said: LOOKING FOR STUDY PARTICIPANTS.

A young oak tree partially obscured the storefront, its branches hanging over the doorframe and window.

All the guy had to do was say "money." Cyrus grabbed his backpack and slushie and hurried after him.

The inside of the place reminded him of a stodgy accountant's office. Instead of shelves and racks full of products to sell, there was just a lonely desk, a laser printer, a telephone, and a back office. In a corner, a giant kennel with cedar shavings, a hamster wheel, and a water bottle hung upside-down with a metal tube. The cage was huge for just a single rat. The man placed the rat in the cage and locked it. He doused his hands with hand sanitizer on the desk, then strode across the gigantic space, grinning with hospitality.

A shiver ran through Cyrus as he stepped onto the threshold of the store. He didn't know how to process the feeling. He paused, looking around.

"Welcome to Whisker & Claw," he said. "I'm Dr. Atticus Thurston."

"Cyrus."

The doctor shook his hand and pulled him into the store.

"You just might be the first Cyrus to walk through this door," the man said. His dark eyes were wild with excitement and friendliness. "Cyrus, the ancient Persian name for Lord. Do you have Persian heritage?"

What kind of question was that?

"Nah, I'm mostly Irish. Little bit of English, I think."

"Ah. I have this game I like to play from time to time to get a sense of people," Thurston said, stroking his beard. "It seems I lost."

So the guy was a doctor. Definitely had the air. A very "holier than thou, but I'll treat you gently" vibe.

"What exactly is this place?" Cyrus asked, looking around again.

He glanced at the rat in the cage.

"Do you sell rats?"

"No."

"Are you guys exterminators?"

"No."

Thurston clucked his tongue as if he had forgotten something. He gestured for Cyrus to wait, and jogged to the back office. He creaked open the door and said a few words softly. A few seconds later, a woman with pigtails and a green sweater emerged with a clipboard, chewing bubblegum.

"We'll see if you're a good fit, Mr. Cyrus. If you are, we'll pay you for your time today, of course. This is Laurel. She has a few interview questions if you don't mind."

Oh boy. Another interview. If this one was anything like

the others, he had about thirty seconds until they threw him out on his ass.

Thurston patted him on the shoulder. "Laurel, will it please you to take care of Mr. Cyrus?"

What kind of dude used "will it please you" in a sentence? Cyrus suppressed a chuckle as the woman said "Of course," and Thurston kissed her on the cheek.

"It was very nice to meet you, Mr. Cyrus," the doctor said. "Don't worry too much about the questions. Even if you're not a fit, we'll pay you for your time today."

With a bow, he retreated to the back office, closing the door softly. In the cage, the rat jumped onto his treadmill.

Cyrus settled into an uncomfortable metal chair at the table with Laurel. She barely acknowledged his existence so far. Just like the other managers. She looked young—too young to be a manager. The Thurston guy was the head honcho.

"Can I have a name for our records?" Laurel asked.

"Cyrus Grant."

She scribbled on her clipboard. The sound of pencils on clipboards was going to trigger him from now on.

"It's not a problem that I look like hell, is it?"

Laurel didn't glance up from her questions. "We've seen worse. Mr. Grant, this is a survey to gauge whether you are a good fit for a research project that Dr. Thurston is working on. As the doctor implied, we may part ways today. Ninety-seven percent of applicants are not a fit for the study."

"With my batting average today so far, you won't hurt my feelings if you tell me to take a hike," Cyrus said, giggling.

Laurel didn't even laugh. At least the other managers had laughed.

"Mr. Grant, the questions I'm going to ask you may seem strange, but please answer them with complete honesty, to the best of your ability."

"As long as you don't ask me about the bank I robbed last night, we'll be good."

Still no reaction. Laurel would make a killer accomplice if he ever decided to commit a crime. She was stone-faced, man...

"Do you believe in ghosts, Mr. Grant?"

He laughed. "I thought you were going to ask me about customer service. What a relief."

Laurel looked up, annoyed. "Do you?"

"Ghosts? No way."

"What about the paranormal and supernatural? Were-wolves, vampires, witches, and the like?"

"God no. They make for great movies, though."

"What is your vision? Do you wear corrective lenses?"

"20/20. I think. And no."

"Do you suffer from claustrophobia?"

"No."

"Arachnophobia—fear of spiders, or katsaridaphobia—fear of cockroaches?"

"Unless they're big enough to beat me up, no."

"Do you mind getting dirty?"

"No."

"Are you afraid of rats, Mr. Grant?"

"Not really. I just don't like it when they brush against my leg when I'm deep in depressing thoughts."

"Yes or no, Mr. Grant."

"No."

Laurel went "hmm" and shrugged. Had it been a good sign? It had to be a good sign!

"Can you swim?"

"Yes."

"On a scale of one to ten, with one being not fearful and ten being fearful, how would you rate visiting a new place for the first time?"

He had to think about that one. "Can you give me an example?"

Laurel popped her bubblegum. "You're in a part of town you don't visit often and make a turn onto a wrong street. You have no idea what's on the other end."

"I'd say a two."

"Would you keep walking down the street or turn around?"

"I guess it depends on the environment. If it's dark, I'm turning around. But if there are people around, I'd check it out. City 101."

"Next question," Laurel said. "Do you like the Teenage Mutant Ninja Turtles?"

"What kind of question is that? Of course."

"If we asked, would you be able to resist making Ninja Turtle jokes? We're a serious operation."

"What the heck are you hiring me to do?"

"The question, Mr. Grant, the question."

"If you pay me enough, sure."

"And one final question. The doctor asks for complete rule-following during the study. You must do everything he asks. Deviation is not tolerated. Will that be a problem?"

"I can follow rules if that's what you're asking."

Laurel set down her pen. "Thank you. Based on your answers, you're a candidate for our study."

"Yes!" Cyrus said, jumping out of the chair and knocking it to the floor. "You have no idea how much I've been wanting to hear a yes today."

Laurel went over the terms with him. He was to report to the Ashland L station tomorrow at seven o'clock, to wear long sleeves and pants, and to come with an enthusiastic personality. More would be shared with him at that time, but the job would pay $15 an hour on a temporary contract.

Cyrus's eyes widened. "You're going to pay me *how* much?"

When Laurel repeated the amount, Cyrus uppercutted the air. It was at *least* a few dollars more than he could have made elsewhere.

"Thank you, thank you, thank you," he said. He pulled out his phone but resisted the urge to text Becca. No, he thought as he skipped out of the store. He'd savor this moment and milk it for as long as he could.

CHAPTER SEVEN

"HE'S A BIT NAÏVE, don't you think?"

From the back office, Thurston spied on the interview and listened through a secret microphone in the ceiling. The window was reflective on the outside, but inside, he could see everything in the store, including Cyrus, who was fidgeting nervously as he answered Laurel's questions.

The only thing that made this stale room bearable was the flowers. The room was covered, quite literally, with flowers. To be among friends as he listened to interviews was the most one could ask for during this dreadful work.

The kid was endearing enough, but his jokes were insufferable.

Thurston leaned back and inhaled the floral scent from a bouquet of night flowers that oriented themselves in Cyrus's direction.

The boutonnière on Thurston's lapel, the acorns wreathed with baby's breath, came alive.

Murgalen's voice whispered, "He's perfect, Atty."

"And why is that again?" he asked, frowning.

"The magic binds better with fools. He's giving the right answers. At this point, it's up to you."

Thurston bit his bottom lip. "It's possible. He could be the final piece."

"Wouldn't he be a nice contrast to the other brute we recruited?" Murgalen asked. "They might not even get along. It could be fun."

Thurston glanced at the clipboard with a bunch of names. What number was Cyrus Grant? How many people had wandered into Whisker & Claw in its various locations across the city? How many of them had contained promise but ultimately disappointed him?

"If you insist," he said. "But he looks just like all the others to me. Empirically, he doesn't check out."

"You and your empiricism," Murgalen said, disgusted. Her voice floated up from the boutonnière. "My magic trumps your scientific *instinct* every time."

Thurston leaned back in his chair. Furrows of displeasure formed on his brow. "If that's true, then why do we keep failing?"

"Magic requires patience," she said. "And trial and error."

"Like science," he said.

"Nothing like science," she said.

Silence.

Cyrus waved good night as he skipped out of the store.

Closing time. Thurston emerged from the office.

A tall, potted laurel tree rested in Laurel's place at the table. Its leaves rustled and swayed, and Thurston snatched the clipboard hanging from one of the branches.

"Thank you, Laurel," he said. He had never quite gotten used to talking to trees and plants, but they always did their work faithfully. The extent of Murgalen's magic never failed to amaze him.

He'd never forget sitting in the alley behind his apartment, after his wife left him, crying and in pain. A flower blew in from the street, drifting on the wind until it landed on his lap.

Then he heard Murgalen's beautiful voice. It came upon him like a gift from heaven.

"They're coming for me," she had told him. "I'm in so much danger."

"Who?" Thurston asked. He would have done anything to protect her. Anything.

"All I wanted to do was heal you," she said. "And they're going to lock me away for my good deed."

"No. They can't."

"Will you do a favor for me?" she asked. "It's just a small favor. But it's based on wisdom I learned from you. You've inspired me so much."

"You've inspired me," he said.

He grunted as he thought about the memory. One long year later, and here he was, trying to free her from the twilight world so that they could be together again. It should've been a crime to lock someone so beautiful away. Still, he didn't know why. He hated being apart from her.

Grabbing his Cubs baseball hat and leather bag off the wall, he nodded to the tree. Then he turned to the corner, to the kennel, where a naked man huddled against the cage, knees pulled into his chest. His body was smeared in dust and dirt and covered in cuts and bruises.

Thurston's face hardened upon seeing the man's pathetic sight.

Donovan Smith, age forty-five, from Avondale. Signed up for a study while waiting for pizza. His biggest hope, and his biggest traitor.

"I did what you told me," Donovan said. "Now let me go."

"You *didn't* do what I told you," Thurston said. "That's why you're here."

"You asked me to find another lost soul," the man said. "I sniffed one out for you. I found you a replacement. So let me go."

"We'll see how he turns out," Thurston said. "Hopefully better than you."

"You turned me into a fucking rat, you bastard," the man said. He shook back-and-forth and began to cry. "A rat!"

Thurston paced the length of the cage. "You put the entire expedition at risk. If you had just listened…"

"And gotten stuck back there with the others? What kind of life is that?"

"You were a coward," Thurston said. "And I have no patience for cowards, or for people who break the rules."

He stopped. "Transform. Now."

Donovan went quiet.

"Transform!" Thurston barked.

Thurston slid an ivory-colored stick from his pocket and pulled it on one side, extending it to two feet with a sharp needle on one end. He drove the point into the man's chest, then his stomach. No blood, but howling pain. Relentlessly, he prodded the man until he cowered at the back of the cage.

Thurston watched with satisfaction as the man shrank, bone and skin molding into chocolate hair, wild whiskers, and pink claws. The rat shivered in the space where the man had been.

Thurston slipped on a pair of latex gloves. Then he pinned the rat to the floor with the poker and produced a sea-green ball the size of a pea from his pocket. He dangled it over the rat's mouth and told it to open up.

The ball disappeared into the rat's throat and Thurston told it to chew and he'd let him go.

When the rat finished chewing, Thurston released the pressure from the poker.

"Out," he said, opening the cage.

The rat jumped out of the cage and toward the door. It raced around the shop madly. Realizing it was free, it shifted. Its hair changed back to flesh and bone and its face bloomed into the man's face again, but midway through the transformation, the man's body jerked violently, a mess of human flesh, whiskers, and eyes dripping like a Dali painting.

Pain and fear flashed in the half rat, half man's eyes, and his tail slapped the floor angrily. He shrank again into a rat.

"Rodenticide laced with magic," Thurston said. He drove the poker into the rat's tail, piercing it. The rat squealed in agony as Thurston carried it through the office and into a back alley. He tossed the rat, and it bounced, landing next to a catch basin where the darkness of a city sewer loomed below. A trickle of blood streaked the asphalt.

Thurston locked the back door. Just like that, it shimmered away, replaced by a brick wall. He tipped his hat to the rat.

"Good night, Donovan."

The rat lay on its side, staring up in fear as Thurston walked past.

The boutonnière came alive again. Murgalen's voice floated through the alley. "Another expensive failure, but I've got a good feeling about the new group, my love."

Thurston stopped and smiled. "If you do, then so do I."

"You don't trust me?"

"Everlastingly," he said as the shadows covered him.

"When we are together again, it all will have been worth it. Shall I sing to you, my love?"

"You know the one," he said, starting the song for her. "Oh, how love lies bleeding in twilight..."

Dr. Atticus Thurston passed onto North Milwaukee Avenue, past the closing shops and the day's remainder of shoppers wandering the sidewalks, whistling along to the song that only he could hear—the one where she sang how much she missed him.

CHAPTER EIGHT

V was for victory!

Outside, Cyrus hopped on his board and picked up speed. He bent his knees and swerved into a V and wove his way down the ramp. Cool evening air swirled past his face, blowing his hair under his helmet.

Now Becca would get off his case. He could make some money and maybe get an apartment of his own soon. Then he could listen to all the bad love songs he wanted and no one would complain.

He liked the ride home—a short, straight shot down North Milwaukee Avenue, where all the historic buildings, restaurants, and streetlights would be coming alive as he passed. Plenty of time to think.

He was cruising now. Only at the last minute when he reached the end of the block did he see a giant raven.

The raven didn't budge.

He bailed, crashing onto the ground, the board narrowly missed striking the bird.

The raven gronked at him. The bird must've had a death wish.

Still, it remained, black feathers reflective in the setting sunlight.

It gronked at him again, flapped its wings, and with a hop, it landed on his board. It was the biggest raven he'd ever seen, and maybe the most beautiful. You almost never saw ravens in Chicago—the place was a crow town. Streaks of blue and purple ran through its feathers, and it stared at him with coal-black eyes. It stood perfectly in the center of the board, like it was ready to ride.

"Hey, get off," Cyrus said, shooing the bird away.

Gronk. Gronk.

The raven landed on a nearby bike loop, revealing a stronger tinge of blue in its wings.

"Rats," the bird said in a hoarse voice.

He jumped at the word.

"Doctor," another voice said.

A second raven flapped down to the hood of a nearby car.

"Doctor. Regret."

"What the—"

"Rats," the first raven said.

"Doctor. Regret," the second raven said.

Cyrus backed away and the ravens extended their wings, gronking in unison, the cords in their throats flexing.

"I'm imagining this," he said softly. "I have to be imagining this."

Suddenly, the Bee Gees crooned from his pocket and his phone buzzed. The ravens scattered.

He stared after the birds as they wheeled over the roof of a nearby shop.

Huh. Even creepy ravens didn't like love songs.

He slipped his earbuds in and took the call from his mom.

"Cyrus Alexander Grant," his mother, Aurora, said sharply.

The only time she used his full name was when he was in trouble. From what he could tell, she was at home, sitting on the back porch, the hum of the Lifetime movies on the TV mixed with parakeet song. The old birds were really squabbling today. She was probably grading unfinished student papers. She taught English at the University of Illinois at Chicago, a half-hour train ride away from Logan Square.

"What did I do?" he asked, jumping on his skateboard. He eased into the street and a car honked at him.

"Are you on that skateboard again?" she asked. "You know I hate that thing."

Cyrus bent down as he coasted through a red light. "It's totally safe, Mom. Lot of crazies on the trains these days. What's up?"

"I was hoping you might tell me. I just received a phone call from Julianeta a few minutes ago."

Cyrus gulped as he rolled between a delivery truck and a motorcycle.

"She says that you've been bothering her," Aurora said. "Is that true?"

"What's your definition of bothering?"

"She says you got into a fight. Are you okay?"

"I'm fine. It's nothing."

"That's not how she described it," Aurora said.

He didn't reply, but his mom didn't accept his silence.

"Well, what did they break?" she asked.

"My pride," he said, pushing through a green light.

"Good. Cyrus, this needs to stop. Now."

Cyrus swallowed hard.

"I'm worried about you," she said, her voice softening. "Becca tells me that you're a nervous wreck. Listening to the Bee Gees every night and crying yourself to sleep?"

"Complete exaggeration," he said. "I haven't cried myself to sleep once."

"But the rest is true?"

"I'm fine, Mom. I just miss her."

"I know," Aurora said. "But there are millions of women in this town. And you're young, handsome, and smart."

"There's only one Jules."

"You have no idea how sweet that is. The next girl will appreciate you so very much. But you need to move on."

A truck cut him off. Quick thinking sent him into oncoming traffic momentarily before he flipped off the driver and gave a hearty *fuck you*. Thank God his mom couldn't see what he was doing.

He safely veered into a left lane, giving the truck a sidelong glance.

"Cyrus?"

"Okay," he said.

"Okay, what?"

"It's over. I'm not going anywhere near her house again. I'll just continue to wallow in my own filth and listen to bad love songs."

"I got you to listen to me for a change. That was a little too easy," Aurora said.

Cyrus stopped at a busy intersection and kicked his board into his hands.

"How's your job search going?" she asked, betraying more of her conversation with Becca.

"Nailed it," Cyrus said. "I start a new gig tomorrow."

"That's fantastic. What is it?"

"A company called Whisker & Claw."

"Sounds hipster," Aurora said. "What do they do?"

"Uh, that's a good question. I'm not sure. They asked me a lot of questions about rats, though."

"Dear God, Cyrus. Pest management is a dirty business."

"It's not that," he said. He jumped on his board and sailed through a green light and into a bike lane. He passed a cyclist on the right.

"Maybe you should ask them more questions," his mom

said. "I love you, but I'm not bailing you out of prison if it turns out to be a shady operation."

Cyrus laughed. "You already deserve sainthood, Mom."

"So does your sister."

"Yeah. Bec is the best."

"You're running her ragged, sweetie. She's more worried about you than I am. Maybe you should get her something."

"Good idea."

He promised to see her soon and told her he loved her before hanging up.

For the rest of the ride, he slipped into a flow, thinking about how the day had turned around. Mom was right. Becca practically had gotten him this job. He thought of the few extra dollars he had in his pocket from the interview. He couldn't help but smile. He stopped at a flower shop on the way home.

As he entered, he didn't notice the pair of ravens circling in the sky above.

CHAPTER NINE

Cyrus had just enough time to get home on his electric skateboard before night fell. He jumped onto the sidewalk in front of Wicked Cat Coffee & Brew, flipping his board into his hands and hooking it on his backpack. He couldn't stop smiling.

He sniffed a bouquet of random flowers that he had stopped to pick up for Becca. Their wet, fragrant smell mixed in with the strong aroma of roasted coffee beans.

Wicked Cat Coffee & Brew was a corner shop with brown and green brick, and windows that served as loading doors that folded up in the summer so people could sit on the patio after dark. Becca's apartment was on the second floor, capped with a historic green turret, the kind that gave the old Chicago buildings flair.

Back in the day, North Milwaukee Avenue in Logan Square was a rough spot. Scary place to go to at night. Lately, the place had been gentrifying, and it was a lot safer. Becca, a hipster at heart who wanted to be in the middle of the city, opened her shop there, as if there weren't a million other coffee shops that the neighborhood was famous for. But even though she was a coffee snob, she was an even bigger beer snob. After dinner, she served microbrews and spiked coffee for all the people who wanted to sober up a bit for before going home. Nothing made Becca happier than wandering her shop with trays of drinks, giving shit to the locals, and not taking shit from anyone at the same time.

He spotted her behind the reclaimed wood counter, under a mason jar light, making what appeared to be one of the last caramel macchiato lattes of the day. A few baristas were rearranging tables and chairs for the night crowd.

He pushed into the shop, and a chime rang over the door.

"I am the champion," he said, holding up his hands in victory. After everyone in the store paused and stared at him, he said, "That is all."

He sat at the bar. A barista with a pompadour hairdo and coffee-stained apron give him a high five. Cristián was one of the original employees that Becca hired when she first opened the shop. He worked the swing shift, and he was equally adept at slinging coffees as well as mixed drinks. The female patrons constantly hit on him too. A Spanish accent would do that. He'd come over from Spain as a foreign exchange student at the University of Illinois at Chicago and ran a photography business on the side.

"Jesus, man," Cristián said.

"Don't ask," Cyrus said.

"Your wish is my command, but Becca will bleed the truth out of you," Cristián said. "And I'm not missing it for the world. Even if it means sacrificing a tip."

Cristián dug a finger into the plastic around the bouquet and pulled them to his nose. "You got me flowers. How sweet."

"You wish," Cyrus said. "I got a new job."

"Let me guess: flower shop?"

"Guess again."

Cyrus spotted a blonde ponytail bobbing around the Wicked Cat in the corner of his eye. Becca served coffee to an elderly couple in front of the window. The bottom of her camo tank was stained with coffee. Then she wandered over. Cyrus handed her the flowers and kissed her on the cheek.

"Who are you and what have you done with my brother?" she asked, skeptical.

"You're looking at the newest employee of the Whisker & Claw Corporation," Cyrus said, grinning. "I walked in and they practically begged me to work there. I'll be working around rats, I think. I'll learn more tomorrow."

"Well, shit. I don't know what to say," she said, sniffing the bouquet. "I was prepared to say something snarky. I stand corrected, Cy."

Then she noticed his eye. "Oh my God, what happened to you?"

"It doesn't matter," he said.

Becca's eyes searched his face. She arched an eyebrow.

"You went to Jules's, didn't you?" she asked. Before he could reply, she hit him several times with the bouquet.

"Oh, come on!" he cried.

Cristián whistled and did a covert slide toward the espresso machine.

"You are such an idiot," Becca said. "When is Jules going to serve you a restraining order?"

"I'm surprised we're not planning your funeral," Cristián said. "Jules's new boyfriend is a muscle factory."

The chime rang over the door, and a duo walked in that stopped the bar. Straight out of the magazines—a man in a leather jacket, white concert t-shirt, and ripped jeans. With him, a blonde-haired woman in a faded flannel shirt with the top two buttons undone, jeans, and brown leather boots.

They stopped as they entered, looking around the shop. Cyrus could smell the guy's cologne from across the shop; he smelled of wintergreen and rubber. A man's man cologne.

Becca called out, "Be with you in a minute." She looked at Cyrus and said, "Thank you for the flowers, and congratulations on the job, but I hope you learned your lesson for once. Cristián, get my brother a drink, on the house…and an ice pack."

Cristián saluted her and said, "One Keystone Ice, coming right up."

"Do it and die," Cyrus said.

Cristián laughed as he squeezed behind the counter with Becca and started mixing a drink.

Cyrus settled down at the table, easing his backpack and skateboard on the floor. He didn't see that the man and woman had sat at the table next to him. They stared, and it startled him.

"Nice wheels," the man said, eyeing his board. "Do you ride a lot?"

"Every day in the spring and summer," Cyrus said. "Unless it's raining."

"I thought about making the investment myself," the man said, "but I'm a motorcycle guy through and through. Nothing will separate me from it."

"Pretty cool," Cyrus said. "Is it outside?"

"We took the train today," the man said. "Luna isn't fond of bikes. Isn't that right, Luna?"

"If I'm going to die, there are better ways," the woman said. She watched Cyrus intently, and her eyes were…mesmerizing. She was taking all of him in, completely concentrating on him, squinting her eyes a little. It made him feel small, yet butterflies in his stomach soared.

"Rocco was so busy admiring your wheels, he didn't see your black eye," she said. "How'd you get that?"

Cristián floated back to the table and slid Cyrus a mixed drink—Becca's Special, cranberry vodka, Sprite, blackberries, and green food coloring, rimmed with crusted salt. He produced an ice pack from his apron, which Cyrus accepted with a grateful nod. Then he blocked him as he took the couple's order. After he walked away, the man smiled at Cyrus and said, "Did you get jumped, bud?"

Rocco glanced over at his female companion and said, "I remember those days."

The woman propped her head on her fists and tilted her head at Cyrus. "I don't. I love a man who knows how to take a fist to the face, though. For a woman, of course."

"I knew there was a reason you were with me," Rocco said, placing his hand on hers. "But seriously, though, you ought to get that eye checked out."

Cyrus held up the icepack to his temple. "It's no big deal."

Rocco shrugged. "Hopefully, it was a good lesson for you. You get those kinds of battle scars, and you try to avoid them in the future. But you don't strike me as the kind that goes around looking for fights."

Cyrus took a sip of his drink. Sweetness exploded across his lips. "You're right."

"Let me guess: it happened over a girl," Luna said.

Cyrus grinned sheepishly.

"I knew it," she said. "Did you clock the other guy?"

"We won't talk about that," Cyrus said.

"Gotcha," the man said. "So you really did get your ass kicked, then."

Cristián returned with a rum and Coke and a tall glass of straight Scotch.

The man raised his Scotch to Cristián and said, "We were just talking to your buddy here about the virtues of self-defense."

Cristián made whiskers with his fingers before heading toward the bar. "Maybe talk to him about self-defense for rats. That's his new job."

"Something like that," Cyrus said, sipping his drink.

"You're a man of mystery," Rocco said. "First, street fights, and then rats, eh?"

Luna sipped her rum and Coke and slid to Cyrus's table. "You've got my attention now, sweetheart."

"It's some job I got today," Cyrus said. "I start tomorrow."

"Congrats," Luna said. "Hopefully, you don't scare easily."

"For the money, I won't."

"Ah, the perennial money issues," Luna said. "We know all about those."

"You don't want to mess around with rats," Rocco said. "Buddy of mine works for the city doing sewer maintenance. Got bit on the hand and ended up in the hospital for a week. Bad infection."

Luna shivered. "I can't imagine. Can we please change subjects?"

"You said you were looking for a job," the man said. "I might know someone who can help you. How'd you like to use your board?"

Cyrus brightened. Sometimes there was a benefit in talking to strangers. You never knew about city life.

"What's the range on your board?" the man asked.

"About seven miles."

"I think that could work," he said, glancing at Luna. "Tell you what. Why don't you come out to Uptown with me tomorrow night? Around dark? I'll give you an address so I can introduce you to a friend of mine. Don't do anything until you've had a chance to talk to her. I think you'll dig what she has to offer."

The time. He was supposed to meet Thurston at the same time.

"That's when I start this new gig," Cyrus said. "Can't we meet earlier? Or the day after tomorrow?"

"She's out of town for a month after tomorrow," Rocco said. "It's gotta be tomorrow, bud."

Cyrus thought about Dr. Thurston and the $15-an-hour paycheck. And then he saw Luna's and Rocco's smiling faces and felt guilty.

"Listen, I really appreciate it, but I already signed a contract," he said, lying. "I don't know you guys."

"Really?" Luna asked. "They made you sign for a job you haven't even started yet?"

Cyrus shrugged.

Rocco took a tall swig of his drink. He dangled the glass, swirling the remainder of the Scotch inside. He looked Cyrus in the eyes. "All right. I get it. You won't reconsider at all?"

"I made a commitment," Cyrus said. He downed the rest of his drink. "It was nice meeting you guys."

Rocco raised his hands in surrender. "I apologize if I came off too strong. I just meet good people and want to help."

"It's why I love him," Luna said.

Rocco nodded. Luna looked away and ran a hand through her hair.

What was up with them? Were they hitting on him? Cyrus couldn't always read people's intentions.

"Good luck, bud," Rocco said, reaching up and patting Cyrus on the back. Cyrus recoiled at the pat.

"Whoa, bud. I didn't mean to scare you," Rocco said. "We wish you all the best."

Cyrus excused himself and headed toward the back of the shop.

"What's with them?" Cristián asked. "They were pretty friendly. Maybe they thought your black eye was sexy."

Cyrus stole another glance at the couple. Rocco and Luna sat, speaking to each other in hushed tones. Rocco noticed and nodded to Cyrus. He chugged the rest of his Scotch and took Luna's hands and caressed them.

"No idea," Cyrus said.

Cristián poked him. "If I didn't know any better, my ménage à trois-dar is going off."

"Get out of here."

"The way she was looking at you and then looking back at him," Cristián said. "Opportunity of a lifetime. They seemed sad that you rejected them. The way he reached up and patted you on the back? That qualifies as a love tap, my friend."

"You're nuts," Cyrus said under his breath.

"Would it be the end of the world?" Cristián asked. "I mean, you're single."

"*You* talk to them, then."

Before he climbed the rear stairs to Becca's apartment, he took a final glance at the couple. Rocco and Luna paid for their tab and left. Once they made it to the sidewalk, Rocco put his arm around Luna and they disappeared into the night.

Cyrus shrugged and went upstairs.

He spent the night thinking about Jules, listening to the Bee Gees, and looking out the window at the blinking traffic lights below.

He fixed himself another Becca's Special from the fridge —she kept the supplies on hand to mix it upstairs if needed.

He sat at the window, swilling the first sip. The patrons from the bar were trickling out of the bar now. A glance at his watch told him it was two o'clock. Closing time.

Boots sounded on the wooden steps approaching the apartment door.

He turned the music off to not irritate Becca. He hurried around, cleaning up a little.

An ear-splitting scream stopped him and made him drop his drink. The glass shattered.

It was Becca.

Cyrus leapt over the couch and whipped open the door, where she was standing in the hallway, pointing at the floor.

Cyrus almost stepped on it with his bare feet but caught himself just in time.

A giant, bloodied rat lay on the doormat.

CHAPTER TEN

CYRUS JUMPED a foot in the air upon seeing the rat.

"How did it get in here?" he asked.

"I don't know, but this is your chance to get some training," Becca said. "Take care of it."

Cyrus stared down at the dying rat. It breathed in and out slowly.

Every hair on his arms stood up. "Why do I have to do it?"

"Hello," Becca said, "you're supposed to be the rat expert."

"Not until tomorrow," he said.

"Will you please just take care of it?" she asked.

Not many things reduced her from tough-as-nails to frightened. Most of the color had drained from her face. "I'm gonna have to call the landlord. We've never had a rat problem before."

"Logan Square is full of rats," Cyrus said. "We had the most complaints in the city last year, remember?"

"But not in this building," Becca said. "I hope they're not downstairs. Can you please do something?"

Cyrus stumbled into the kitchen. "I'm not touching that thing with my bare hands!" he called back.

"Get some tongs," Becca said, her voice more distraught. "And a container. Put some gloves on, for Christ's sake!"

Cyrus paused and glanced around the kitchen. "Where are they?"

"You've lived with me two weeks and you still don't know where anything is," Becca cried. "Drawer next to the refrigerator, doofus!"

Cyrus pulled on two oversized rubber gloves. Then he opened all the drawers one by one in quick succession. He found a pair of tongs and an oversized salad bowl.

"You're not ruining the salad bowl that Mom gave me for Christmas," Becca said, folding her arms. "Find another container."

"Then YOU take care of it," Cyrus said, grabbing a spaghetti colander instead.

He stood over the rat. The body loomed larger, though it must've been his mind playing tricks on him. He couldn't imagine touching it.

The rat looked Satanic. Clotted blood covered a wound at the base of its tail. Its mouth was open, bright yellow incisors on the top and bottom showing—a visage from a nightmare. Its beady black eyes stared into nothingness.

"I haven't done this in forever," Cyrus said. "Not since we lived in that little apartment when we were kids."

"Don't remind me," Becca said.

Cyrus reached down with the tongs, but then he recoiled. "This is crazy."

"You can do it, Cy," Becca said. "Or I'm putting you out on the street tonight. I take back everything I said."

"Thanks for the confidence boost," he said. He took a deep breath, looking at the rat again.

He could do this. He could do it!

In one fluid motion, he grabbed the rat's body with the

tongs, but tripped, and the rat bounced across the floor, hit the wall, and landed face-down. He dropped the tongs and crashed against the wall, jumping away from the rat in fright.

Becca screamed again.

"You suck!" she shouted.

Cyrus sighed and grabbed the rat again with the tongs. This time, he had a firm grip.

Screw the colander! He threw it aside and bolted down the stairs.

With one hand, he pushed open the security door that separated the hallway from the foyer from the private residence. He wouldn't allow himself to breathe.

He burst through the front door, into the night air, bare feet on cold asphalt, and around the building into the alley behind the Wicked Cat.

He beelined for the dumpster. The lid was closed and he cursed at the revelation.

Holding the tongs in one hand and reaching for the dumpster lid with the other, he tried to lift the lid and toss the rat in. But he lost his balance and misjudged his aim, and the animal struck the side of the dumpster like a brick and rolled underneath.

He cringed.

Hopefully, Mother Nature would take care of it for him. He'd had enough of rats for one night.

He slipped off the gloves and threw them into the dumpster quickly, afraid that the rat would somehow come to life and bite him on the ankle.

Then he heard a squeak.

The damned rat was alive. And it was squeaking at him!

He tore out of the alley, nearly stumbling, his feet covered in grime and gravel. Only when he was safely inside the building did he exhale.

Upstairs, Becca had the hallway floor doused in bleach and was mopping it up. She had gone a little overboard and covered her mouth with her starry night bandanna. Cyrus coughed upon smelling the odor.

"Did you take care of it?" she asked, her voice muffled.

Cyrus thought of the rat underneath the dumpster and decided not to tell Becca that his aim had been bad. He just nodded.

"Well, if you get a chance tomorrow," she said, "see if you can bring some rat poison home with you from your new job. If customers find out that we have rats, I'm screwed. God, I'm so screwed."

She was rattled. Cyrus took the mop from her. "Why don't you finish up downstairs?" he asked. "I'll take care of it."

Becca composed herself and jogged back to the shop, tying her bandanna in a haphazard knot across her head.

As he mopped the floor, Cyrus couldn't get the image of the rat out of his head—brown hair, streaks of black, long tail. He got the sense that he'd seen it before, but there were hundreds of thousands of rats in the city. Then he finished cleaning up, put his pajamas on, and went to bed.

He dreamt of rats.

To a soundtrack of a heartbeat, he walked through a graffiti-filled alley and oval shadows darted out in crisscrossing patterns before him. He startled.

Reflective eyes stared at him from inside a sewer grate. He stepped on a manhole and heard squabbling down below. Something brushed against the manhole's lid from below, threatening to push it up.

Cyrus jumped over it and started to run. Suddenly, claws scratched all over his skin, all over his body.

Rats. All over him.

He screamed, pulling at his skin, but the rats dug in, staring at him and shrieking.

He fell on his back and found, conveniently, a pair of tongs on the ground. One by one, he plucked the brown rats off of him like burrs, casting them into the sewer. He ran like hell until he reached the end of the alley, where a brick wall awaited him. He turned around, seeing the rats' eyes in the darkness. They were climbing out of the sewer in bigger numbers now.

The heartbeat continued as the rats consumed the alley—scratching, squabbling, shadows zipping along the walls.

It all stopped when someone tapped him on the shoulder.

His mom. Long brown hair with streaks of gray, navy blue sundress, and a sleek black purse over her shoulder. His mom was what Becca would look like when she was older, with slight wrinkles and graying hair. She had a CD in her hand. The Bee Gees. The Gibb brothers stared at him, hairy man chests exposed through white leisure suits.

"I've been looking for you everywhere, sweetheart," she said. "I thought you might like this. Don't tell Becca I gave it to you."

And suddenly, he felt Becca's presence, even though she wasn't there with him. She was going to be angry at the CD. "No more Bee Gees!" he could hear her say.

"I'm in mortal danger and you give me a CD?" he asked incredulously.

"What danger?" Aurora asked. She turned and beheld the alley, which was now filled with flowers and bright as a summer's day. The walkway was covered in a patchwork of concrete and grass.

"But the rats—"

His mom was gone. The brick wall behind him was gone too, replaced by a street and a park. Logan Square Park, the one right in front of the Wicked Cat. It was a small island in the middle of several busy streets, with a street cutting right through it like a ribbon. But the roads were quiet; a lone car swirled past in an ethereal wisp. The park's giant Greek pillar monument with an eagle perched at the top stood tall over the trees, a brilliant gray against the the swaying tree-tops and stars.

He smelled Becca's telltale coffee. He even heard her voice and her full-throated laugh. Through thick bushes and oak tree leaves, he sensed her, though the foliage obscured his sight of the coffee shop save for the fringes of light around the shop's windows.

He dug his hands into his pockets and crossed the street into the park. Above the tall trees, he heard something jangling, like wind chimes.

In the azure sky, he saw himself in double exposure. His head, rising and rising, looking up into the sky, the entire park and square within him. Higher up, distant in the pure blue sky, were twinkling stars. His head inhaled, filling the air with the sound of jangling. His shoulders shook the oaks as they rose over the tops of the buildings.

"Becca?" Cyrus called.

But she didn't respond.

"Bec!" Cyrus said again, growing more nervous.

He walked into the park and into the depths of his rising soul.

CHAPTER ELEVEN

"MISS GRANT, everybody has rats. It's Chicago."

A burly exterminator in a white jumpsuit stared curiously at Becca and Cyrus as they stood on the sidewalk outside the Wicked Cat. He had a bushy mustache and a paunch. An embroidered company logo on his chest said "Fontanelli & Son Pest Control." The logo was an angry brown rat, a cockroach, and a spider in a giant crosshair. Cyrus wondered if this guy was Fontanelli himself or the son.

"Call me next time you see a rat and I'll come out as soon as possible."

Cyrus sensed the heat from Becca rising like a thermometer. She wasn't going to take "no rats" for an answer. They'd already waited all day for him to show up, which he did just before the evening rush, and that didn't help Becca's stress levels.

The exterminator crossed something off his clipboard, and Cyrus wanted to wince. Clipboards...no more clipboards...

Fontanelli wrinkled his bushy mustache and said, "I looked all over the perimeter. I didn't see a thing. You got rats in the alley, sure. Everybody does. The dumpsters are like smorgas-bord buffets for them. But you do an okay job in the coffee shop, so they stay outside. Same time next month?"

Becca didn't say anything. The wind blew, rustling her bandanna, and she stared daggers at the exterminator.

"Wait a minute," Cyrus said, buying the guy some time before his inevitable bend to his sister's will. "The rat wasn't in the coffee shop. It was outside the apartment. You didn't see anything up there?"

"I know rats," the exterminator said. "It doesn't follow that any were up there. There's no food. The doors are sealed. Sure, they could get in if they wanted to, but you folks don't strike me as slobs. Your apartment was squeaky clean aside from some plates in the sink." He shrugged. "And I'm just as guilty of that as you, fella."

"Obviously, it didn't get in my apartment because it was lying dead on my welcome mat," Becca said, dismissing Cyrus's question. "If there's a rat, there are likely more we can't see. And if I have a problem downstairs, I want to be proactive. So I need your help, please."

Becca always put please at the end of a command. In Cyrus's case, it meant he needed to do it. If he didn't, he would die. No telling what she would do to this guy.

Fontanelli frowned. "Listen, Miss Grant. You're a great customer. I see you twice a month and I appreciate your busi-ness. But I don't believe in fixing what isn't broken."

Becca said nothing.

"How do you know it wasn't a cat that drug it in?" Fontanelli asked.

"There aren't any cats in the building," she said, dismissing him. "I already checked that."

"Dogs?"

"Someone does have a dog, yes."

"See, that's it," Fontanelli said. "I could treat your building with extra traps and rodenticide. But it's not to solve the problem, because you ain't got a problem. All it's going to do is cause trouble for the other pets in your nice facility."

"You've got to be kidding me," she said. "We know what we saw. How do you explain it, then?"

Fontanelli looked up at the apartment window for a moment, thought, and shook his head. "Maybe the thing was poisoned to the point that it got disoriented. When rats eat poison, they don't die right away. They wobble their way to death. We call it dead rat walkin'. Maybe one of your people left the back door to the alley open. The rat gets in, but he's already poisoned, see. He's not exactly making smart decisions. Somehow he ends up on your doorstep, and boom—you call me."

"That's ridiculous," Becca said.

"You ain't made any enemies?" Fontanelli asked. "Angry boyfriend?"

"No."

"Know any witches?" Fontanelli asked.

"Witches aren't real," Becca said.

"Then like they say in the priesthood: it beats the hell out of me."

"Fine," Becca said. "I understand what you're saying, but you have to understand where I'm coming from."

"I've been honest with you for the last two years. Why would I lie to you?" Fontanelli tapped his watch. "I got a hundred other clients, half of them in Logan Square. You know how many calls I get? You know how many times I have to go to the same residence and explain to customers the same things over and over again, that they ain't got a rat problem, that they got a human problem? I tell 'em—use a dumpster like you're supposed to, with the lid closed. Don't leave food out. Caulk your openings. I've been doing this for thirty-seven years and I can tell you plenty of stories. But I guarantee you won't find any exterminator in this city that can give you a story about how that rodent ended up on your doorstep, ma'am."

Cyrus whispered to Becca, "Maybe he's right."

The exterminator wandered to the back of his work van and opened up the rear doors. Checking his inventory, he nodded and walked back over to them. "Here's what I'll do. I'll put a few extra traps out in strategic spots. If you have rats inside, and I mean IF, we'll catch one or two. I won't even have to charge you for my time today. But if I don't catch any in the next week, then I'm gonna have to charge you."

Becca extended a hand. "Deal."

"All right, I'll get to work."

Cyrus and Becca waited while Fontanelli worked in the back of the van, preparing snap traps and poison.

"You think he'll catch anything?" he asked.

"God I hope so," Becca said, returning to the coffee shop.

Cyrus's phone beeped in his pocket.

His alarm.

It was time to leave so that he could meet Thurston. But maybe Fontanelli could give him some rodent tips.

"Excuse me, sir?" Cyrus asked.

Fontanelli, probably irritated from doing Becca this favor when he could have been at other paying jobs, peeked out from behind the door of the work van. Bright green balls reflected from a white tub. Fontanelli was scooping them into a bucket.

"Is there anything I should know about…working with rats?" Cyrus asked.

"Huh?"

"I got this job," Cyrus said, "and I don't really know what to expect. All I know is that we're going to be working with rats. Wild ones, I think."

"Be sure to hug 'em," Fontanelli said, "and kiss 'em on the

mouth while you're at it." Fontanelli looked him up and down. "Did you get beat up by a rat? You should take care of that eye, champ."

Cyrus puffed sarcastically and walked away.

CHAPTER TWELVE

THE JOB SITE was too far for Cyrus to ride his skateboard, so he took the Blue Line downtown and transferred to the Orange Line at Clark and Lake. He watched wistfully outside as the train circled around the heart of downtown before traveling south, away from the city, past factories, abandoned warehouses, tall rectangular Chicago homes surrounded by wavering mature trees, the Stevenson Expressway that reminded him of a Celtic knot, and across the Chicago River and to the Ashland Station.

The station sat right on the river, parallel to freight train tracks and a steel drawbridge covered in graffiti.

He walked out onto the platform, down a tiled stairwell, and out of the station into a two-way bus loop.

The place was outdated and smelled of sweat, exhaust, and raw heat from the tracks above. Rush hour foot traffic was thinning out, and only a few people were waiting around for the next bus. The sky had a brownish haze to it, and he could see the air swirling in places. Above, storm clouds rolled in slowly over the city. He patted the umbrella hooked to his backpack to make sure it was still there.

He looked around. No sign of Thurston.

He gulped. There were some places in Chicago you just didn't go unless you had a reason to. And even then...

All the people in the station were Asian or Latino. He became supremely aware of the fact that he was one of the only white dudes around. The place was gritty but not necessarily unsafe. But after sundown? No freaking idea, and he considered calling a ride share home. The trains would be way too dangerous after midnight.

At least he was getting paid. Hopefully not cash. Damn it, why didn't he think of this yesterday? He'd be walking around with a wallet flush with money. His mom's voice echoed in his head.

Footsteps approached him from behind, making him turn around.

A balding white guy in a faded blue sweatshirt and sweatpants waddled to him.

Cyrus took a step backward. The guy wore a taut, military style backpack. He could've swung the thing off like a weapon. His cheeks were pouchy, and he had a patch of freckles under one eye, and fiery red stubble.

Cyrus grabbed the straps of his backpack. He didn't want to get jumped again.

"Let me guess: Whisker & Claw," the man said, leveling a finger at Cyrus.

A wave of relief washed over Cyrus. "Yeah, that's me."

The man grinned. "I figured as much. The old doctor wasn't playing around when he told us to show up with an enthusiastic mindset, was he?"

"Any idea what we're supposed to be doing?" Cyrus asked.

"Something about rats," the man said. "Where'd the doc find you?"

"Logan Square. You?"

"Not far from here. He ask you a buncha funny-ass questions?"

"The one about the ninja turtles?" Cyrus asked.

They shared a laugh.

"I'm Zane."

"Cyrus."

"We're in for some shit, ain't we, Cyrus? Just as long as we're getting paid, I'm good with it."

A voice sounded from behind them. "If you have any complaints or reservations about this place, blame Laurel, not me."

Dr. Atticus Thurston approached, smiling wide and pulling an oversized gray suitcase behind him. He carried several shovels tied together with a rope. He looked like a tourist—not someone you saw around these parts that often. The doctor wore a windbreaker and straight jeans that gave off an "out of touch dad" vibe.

Two more people trailed him—a black woman with twist-outs who eyed the station suspiciously and an Asian man about Cyrus's age with messy black hair and frightened eyes.

"You're all shockingly punctual," Thurston said. "And for that, I thank you."

The Asian man looked around. "We're working here?"

"No, Henry, we walk," the doctor said enthusiastically. He distributed the shovels, and Cyrus patted his against his shoulder. The group followed him as he crossed a busy street and walked alongside a food distribution center where delivery trucks bustled to and from loading bays.

A few turns later, they were walking along a wrought-iron fence overgrown with vegetation. An enormous cement silo complex rose into the sky above the trees, covered in graffiti at the top. The storm clouds framed the silos, and the whole scene was like an Instagram photo with a brown filter over it. Cyrus had heard of the place, but he had never been there.

"You're not taking us to the Damen Silos, are you?" the black woman asked.

"That's our destination, Jenae," Thurston said.

"No one can go in there," Jenae said. "It's illegal."

"You are correct," Thurston said.

The group paused. Cyrus and Zane exchanged a confused glance as a car sped past.

Thurston produced a paper from the inner pocket of his windbreaker and snapped it loose. It had the seal of the City of Chicago at the top. He handed it to Jenae, who read the paper with surprise.

The paper passed among the group, Cyrus last.

Cyrus read the paper but didn't understand it. The words glided across his vision, but he couldn't comprehend them.

"Is that satisfactory?" Thurston asked.

Everyone in the group nodded, unsure of themselves.

"I don't get people arrested," the doctor said. "Too much of a liability."

He started walking again, and the group followed.

They reached a dilapidated chain-link fence with a long rectangular sign that said STATE PROPERTY. NO TRES-PASSING.

As they approached the fence, Thurston took off his wind-breaker and wrapped it around his waist. The boutonnière was pinned to his shirt, and it flapped in the breeze.

A horn honked and a voice shouted, "Stop right there!"

A white pickup truck with a green light on the cab barreled into the driveway, skidding to a stop at the fence. A security guard in a blue uniform rocketed out of the car.

"I'm calling the police. Stay right there. All of you."

"There's no need for that," Thurston said. "I have special permission from the city to enter this premises."

"Bullshit," the guard said, pulling out his phone.

Thurston had a word with the man, showing him the permit. The doctor spoke softly, and Cyrus couldn't hear him. Immediately, the guard walked to the fence, unlocked it, and told them to be careful.

Cyrus, Henry, Jenae, and Zane were incredulous as the guard closed the gate behind them.

"How long do you folks need?" the guard asked.

Thurston said something, almost hummed it. The guard nodded.

They walked uphill toward the giant silos. One of the stacks faced them, with a tall, narrow stairwell on one side facing the river, windows wearing graffiti like eyebrows. The other stack sat perpendicular to it, and beyond it, a burnt-out husk of a warehouse.

The place was colored with graffiti. Everywhere. The tops and bottoms of the silos. The warehouse. At least a thousand urban explorers had left their unsavory mark on this place, all trying to one-up each other. Cyrus wondered what all the symbols and letters meant.

Thurston set the suitcase on the gravel ground and unlatched it, revealing a cluster of hardhats stacked on each other, work gloves, orange safety vests, headlamps, and knee pads.

"Did you know that a team of rats is called a mischief?" he asked. "That's a lot cooler than a murder of crows, if you ask me."

Thurston handed out the safety equipment and told everyone to put it on. He paced around, making sure that everyone wore it correctly before putting on his own.

"You look like a group that's ready to work," he said.

With the hardhat strapped to his head, Cyrus felt like a little boy playing a grown-up's game. He'd never worn a safety vest before, and it hung loosely on him. Becca would have laughed at him; no, she would have keeled over and not been able to stop laughing. He could hear her voice now. "Hey, guys, look at me. I'm so adorkable!" Even though he was imagining it, he bristled at her teasing.

Jules would've thought he looked sweet. She would've cocked her head to the side, smiled, and taken his cheeks with both hands, saying, "You look so handsome." And she would've kissed him, giving him some confidence. But here he was, all alone, no one to share this moment with except for strangers just as nervous and afraid as him.

"I'm so glad that all of you joined me today," Thurston said. The group gathered in a semi-circle. Through a road between the silos, the city skyline lay shrouded in the distance with the white tips of the Willis Tower blinking against the belly of the clouds. A crisp breeze blew across the complex.

"I suppose I should tell you what I've hired you to do," Thurston said.

Cyrus gulped.

Thurston glanced at each of the participants for a few seconds. "We are simply here to reclaim something that I've lost. What I'm asking you to do is quite simple: search and find."

Confusion spread across the black woman's face. "Why can't you go in there and find it yourself?"

"That's a very good question, Jenae. I will be searching right along with you. But my medical condition prevents me from doing the most strenuous work. That's why I need you healthy people to help me."

"What exactly are you looking for, boss?" Zane asked. "Rats?"

"We'll talk about rats later," Thurston said. "I'm looking for a pathway. These silos used to store the city's grain. Built at the turn of the last century, they stood as an emblem of Chicago's power. They sat at the junction of city, railroad, and river. As you can imagine, grain dust is quite flammable, and so the place suffered from explosions. A final explosion in '77 put the silos out of commission for good."

Thurston stared at the silos, wonder in his eyes. "Now nature has reclaimed what man built. It has hollowed out our center of power."

"Great history lesson," Cyrus said, "but I'm still confused about what you need us to do."

"That's the thing about rats," the doctor said. "To understand them is to understand history. Imagine what kind of heyday they had, feeding off the grain in the basements. I can only surmise that this place was completely, hopelessly, and dangerously infected with rats."

He turned to the group and laughed.

"Underneath the silos are a series of tunnels," Thurston said. "My understanding is that there is an old substructure beneath *that*. If that's true, then that's where we'll find our rats, rats who have probably never seen man since the days of plentiful grain."

They walked across the silo grounds, shoes crunching gravel, trash, and weeds.

"The convergence of past, future, present, and the one thing that we seem to forget—nature," Thurston said. "This place fed the entire city of Chicago. Hard to believe."

Thurston led them to a ragged concrete maw at the bottom of one of the silos. They climbed through.

Cyrus slid down a hill of sand. Dirt flitted around him and he coughed. He stood, but he was up to his ankles in trash.

The maw let in a dust-sparkled ray of light that lit up the circular room covered in graffiti and trash. A river of mud flowed from a coiled pipe in the corner. The place smelled wet, as if the water had nowhere to go, standing for days and days. He slapped away a mosquito.

A pit opened up in Cyrus's stomach. He sensed Henry and Jenae breathing next to him.

"Headlamps on," Thurston said.

Cyrus activated his headlamp, still feeling like he was the oddball out in the group. The graffiti-smeared walls came into sharper view.

Thurston grabbed his shoulder. "You okay?"

"I'm fine."

"There's nothing to worry about," Thurston said. "Urban explorers come here all the time. But they aren't going to see what we will. If it makes you feel any better, there've only been a few deaths at the site. From time to time, adventurers wander up into the silos and fall down the shafts. You'd have to be stupid to climb the fire escapes here. They're liable to collapse. Fortunately for us, our work today is subterranean, where it is perfectly safe."

If he had been trying to cheer Cyrus up, mentioning people dying didn't help. But at least he wouldn't have to worry about the heights. He followed Jenae and Henry down into the darkness, Thurston behind him.

Their headlamps illuminated a long, gloomy tunnel. Asymmetric doorways made the tunnel look as if it were floating, as if you were looking at it with your head tilted even though you were standing upright. Rays of slanted evening light cut the tunnel into diagonal, cemented shards of graffiti.

The first thing Cyrus noticed was the smell of human shit.

"God, it stinks," he said.

Henry and Jenae wrinkled their noses in disgust as well.

"I've smelled worse, buddy," Zane said.

Thurston was unfazed. "Stay straight down this tunnel until you reach the ray of light at the end."

They marched through the tunnel, through trash and unspecified debris, past darkened rooms that could have been lived in. Cyrus had read articles in the newspaper about urban explorers who were attacked by vagrants. He sure hoped they wouldn't run into anyone here.

Ahead, Zane stopped. "Next steps, boss?"

"Whoa," Henry said, shining a flashlight on a mural of a man performing cunnilingus on a woman. The woman's head arched back in pleasure. Unintelligible words in blood red surrounded her hair like a halo. For some reason, Cyrus couldn't stop looking at it until Henry shone his headlamp on his face. "It's like an unofficial graffiti museum."

Cyrus peeked into a darkened square. He swept his flashlight in and jumped at the sight of a large potted tree.

"Who put this tree down here?" he asked.

Zane shone his flashlight on the tree. "People are weird."

"Here's the spot," Thurston said. "Let's start digging."

Thurston dug his shovel into a mound of dirt in the middle of the room, carried it into the hallway, and dumped it.

"I want this floor clean," he said. "Clean as can be expected given the environment."

Cyrus followed suit. He scooped his shovel into the footprint-covered dirt and carried it into the hallway.

Soon, they reduced the mound to a flat film on the floor. Thurston got down on his knees and scooped away the remaining dirt with his gloves, revealing a circular drain covering with a diameter about three feet across.

"Found it," Thurston said. "Storm drain."

"You want *us* to go down *there*?" Jenae asked. "Uh uh."

"The old workers used to access the grains from the spigots in the ceiling," Thurston said, pointing to the shadowed, riveted slope in the ceiling. "But they had to clean the place out from time to time. Hence the drains. My intuition was spot on. Zane, you first."

"What are we going to find down there ?" Henry asked.

Thurston grinned. "We'll learn out together, Henry."

Cyrus put his hands on his hard hat as Zane climbed down rusty metal steps into deep darkness. Jenae followed him reluctantly as he promised that he'd be the one to die first if things came down to it.

Henry and Cyrus exchanged glances as if to say "this is crazy." But then Henry was climbing down after Jenae.

Then it was Cyrus's turn. Thurston motioned for him and helped him onto the ladder.

He lowered himself onto the ladder. Zane's voice echoed from below.

"I made it," Zane said.

Jenae also made it to the bottom of the pit.

Cyrus opened his mouth to make a joke, but the step underneath him sheared away from the wall.

Henry cursed below. Jenae screamed.

Cyrus instinctively swiped up toward Thurston and yelled his name.

Thurston reached down with concern on his face, but Cyrus's hand missed his. Then the cylindrical darkness flipped up from under Cyrus and he fell.

CHAPTER THIRTEEN

Cyrus's backpack—and Henry—broke his fall.

They lay in a drain, tangled in each other.

Four hands pulled them apart—Jenae and Zane.

"You okay?" Jenae asked, Cyrus's headlamp shining on her face.

Cyrus felt his arms and legs. Nothing broken. Thank God.

Zane was nearby, looking up into the well.

"I'd say we're fucked," Zane said. "The middle set of steps are unstable and unmoored from the wall. Well, Doc?"

"Is everyone okay?" Thurston asked.

"We're fine," Cyrus said. "Luckily, we didn't fall too far."

He swept his light across the drain. It was pitch black down here, and barely enough room for them to stand upright. His shoes sloshed in sticky mud and water. The stale air stunk like decomposing waste and old rainwater.

"I'll call for help," Thurston said. "The guard should still be there. But while you're down there, please explore. I want a report of what you see."

They waited in silence, adjusting to the shadows. Cyrus heard Thurston's voice above. He was talking to someone, probably on his phone. The sound gave Cyrus comfort. Help would be on the way soon.

"You heard the doctor," Zane said, charging ahead into the unknown.

"Definitely a sewer system," Cyrus said, shining a light on the paved bricks that made up the curved tunnel.

Together, they plunged into the muddy darkness.

Thurston quietly slid the drain cover shut.

How many had fallen for the same old trick?

"I trust you'll mend the steps like last time, Laurel," he said to the tree in the room next door.

"Listen, this is Dr. Atticus Thurston," he said suddenly. "I'm in the basement at the Damen Silos. Several of my employees are trapped in a drain. I need immediate help. STAT!"

His voice echoed through the empty chambers.

Waiting a moment, he said, "Yes, I have permission to be here, you idiot! I merely allowed my lover to glamour everyone into letting me in here. Now, will you or won't you send someone to help, please?"

The word "please" echoed until the final cement wall cut it short.

"Well, if you won't help me, then they'll have to fend for themselves," he said. "You'll never live it down!!"

Hearing his work sufficient, Thurston leaned over the drain.

"They're coming!" he cried. "I'll call you when they arrive!"

"Got it," Cyrus said, his voice distant.

Thurston sighed with relief and sat against the wall. His boutonnière hummed to life.

"Atty, you outdid yourself again," Murgalen said.

"Do you think they will finish it?"

"I know they will," she said. "Our time is now."

"Two years paying your penance," he said.

"Two years of solitude," she said. "For love."

"For love."

"I'll handle it from here, my love."

He closed his eyes and rested his head on the wall as his sweet woman began to sing.

"Do you hear that sound?" Cyrus asked.

They stopped.

A voice floated to them from the darkness.

A woman.

A woman was singing.

La de da de la la la...

"Jenae, if that's you, then you win," Henry said. "I'm going to crap my pants and it's the most epic joke ever."

"It's not me," Jenae said quickly, at the same time the voice sang.

Everyone stopped.

Cyrus was going to be sick.

The woman's song was like an opera singer's—long, mellifluous. He had never heard anything so beautiful. Like a woman sitting on her window sill in the middle of a busy city, singing the song on her heart.

"Where is it coming from?" Zane asked. "Ahead or behind?"

Cyrus listened. "Can't tell," he said.

"We're stuck with no place to run," Jenae said. "And it's getting closer."

The voice intensified.

La de da de la la la...how love lies bleeding in twilight...

Cyrus's headlamp lit up something on the wall. A line.

He touched it, and it crumbled in his glove.

Was it...a vine?

His headlamp illuminated an object wedged between the bricks. He squinted and inspected it.

A dead flower. Its color was washed out in the bright lamp. But he plucked the petals off.

"What the—?"

"Why are there mushrooms down here?" Zane asked.

They stood back to back, sweeping their headlamps across the muddy floor. Amidst the mud were brown, spongy mushrooms ribbed like tripe and covered with white liver spots. The mushrooms surrounded them in a circle, and the edges of the circle began to smoke and gray, emitting spores of light.

A spore drifted in front of Cyrus's face, then faded.

All the while, the woman's voice grew louder.

The circle burned blue-hot, flashing around them.

Cyrus wanted to run. Back into the darkness. Back into the mud.

But all he could do was open his mouth to cry for help as the circle roared to life and swept him away in a column of white, milky light.

CHAPTER FOURTEEN

"Cyrus, there's no need to close your eyes."

Cyrus uncoiled from a fetal position at the sound of a woman's voice. He was floating in a swirl of orange and yellow. The world was soup around him.

"Do not be afraid," the woman said. Her voice was soft.

"Where am I?" he asked.

"Where you are matters less than where you're going," she said. "Or is it that you're going nowhere?"

The voice seemed to spin around him, fooling his ears on an exact location.

"You are in the land of the fae," she said after a brief pause.

"Fae?"

"Faeries, my dear. Haven't you heard of them?"

"Like Tinkerbell?"

"We do not speak of that bitch here," the woman said. "Besides, she doesn't exist. I speak of beings who are the manifestation of nature. We inhabit the rivers, rocks, and trees. We have lived with humans side by side for years, passing through to the mortal world without their knowing."

Cyrus shook his head. He had to be dreaming or suffering the side effects of a drug.

"You have intrigued me," she said. "Ever since I sensed you, your spirit has intoxicated me. I can't stop thinking about you. The *idea* of a man like you, Cyrus Alexander Grant. You are so different from the other lost souls."

"Lost souls? Screw you."

"I have seen the depths of your soul," the woman said. After a pause, she said, "If you weren't lost, you wouldn't be here. You'd be back at home with your beloved sister and beautiful Jules."

How did she know all of this? Why did she have to bring Becca and Jules into this?

"You are hopelessly in love with a broken heart," the woman said. "It saved your life."

Her voice took on a tinge of coldness now, like sharp rain.

"I could have broken your heart and left you strewn after me like a junkie always chasing a high," she said. "But your heart belongs to another. So you will be useful to me in other ways."

"Let me out of here," he said. "I'll be useful to no one except myself."

"Cyrus, this is the end of the road for you. Your life wouldn't have had much meaning anyway."

"You're going to kill me?" he asked.

"Not death, my love. Life. Your soul travels down a new path today, and I, Murgalen, the mighty goddess, am your maker."

"I just want to go home," Cyrus said.

"I will allow you to return home. But first, I have a demand. I will send you back to your mortal life in exchange for one deed."

"I don't have a choice, do I?"

"Very good, human."

The way she said "human" chilled him. What did a fae look like?

"Things are going to be different from now on, but don't be afraid. This is just part of the new you, Cyrus."

He felt his body shrinking, his center of gravity diminishing. His eyes shook in their sockets, his skin crawled and stretched in places as if someone were pulling him apart with a thousand clothespins. Ripples of pain dug into his bones. Something...was growing out of his ass. Or was his ass lengthening? And his legs—a crooked claw sprouted from both his hands, and his fingers fused into it. Claws grew from his feet, and his toes snapped together as if they were breaking. And then his nose grew like Pinocchio's. It inched forward from his face, his skin molding itself into a triangle tipped with the flesh-colored snout. But the worst was his mouth. His teeth busted loose from his gums, curves straightening into molars. Down from his triangular face, two long incisors grew like stalactites in a time-lapse; two incisors rose from his lower jaw, snapping into place. And then, as if invisible hands plucked them from his head—whiskers.

He opened his mouth to scream, but a feeble squeak escaped instead.

His torso ballooned into a hump, and something slapped it. A tail—did he have a tail?

His body stopped shrinking, and for the first time, he breathed in, air rushing into little lungs.

The orange world that enveloped him was a pear-colored, muted green now. Had it changed color? Or was it him?

The woman spoke again, but this time, her voice was louder, deeper, multidimensional. It was like someone flipped the switch and gave him three-dimensional ears. Her voice was still just as beautiful as ever, but the coldness he heard earlier was intensified. He sensed... emotion. Love, hatred, callousness, and—deeply distant but pulsing like an undertone —fear.

And he smelled her—oh, how he smelled her. She reminded him of wet grass after rain, dirt infested with worms, a meadow of roses, and—a mixture of scents that he didn't understand logically but knew primally: sweat, sex, and wet bark.

"My dear Cyrus," she said. "Don't be afraid."

He opened his mouth to say "what have you done to me?" But all that escaped was a series of shrieks. He beheld his claws, but they were blurry.

"Your new path begins now," she said.

Cyrus squeaked.

"Cyrus, you're a rat," she said.

CHAPTER FIFTEEN

Becca Grant wiped down the bar as the last patrons tottered out of the Wicked Cat. Her hands smelled of bleach as she set her rag aside. She poured herself a drink, tears in her eyes. The ultramodern furnishings of the coffee shop and bar she had built from the ground up blurred before her. She took the rag and threw it at the front window with rage.

It had been three months since Cyrus disappeared. She had left him on the sidewalk in front of the Wicked Cat after arguing with Fontanelli. She hadn't even told him good luck. She was so irritated with Fontanelli that she couldn't think straight. She had never forgiven herself for it.

She couldn't even hug her brother and tell him good luck on the very job that *she* had made him take?

She regarded her bitter beer.

She hadn't even asked him where he was going. Where the hell was he even going to work anyway?

When Cyrus didn't come home that night, she was a little concerned but not entirely worried. It was unlike him not to come home, but if it was really late, he might have gone to Mom's because she was centrally located in the city and easier to get to, especially from downtown. Plus, even though Logan Square had come a long way, it could be a little scary after midnight.

But when her mom answered the next morning and said nothing of Cyrus, fear struck her. Aurora wasn't happy with her either.

An online search for the "Whisker & Claw Corporation" turned up nothing online. All she found were dog and cat grooming companies, all in Minnesota and California.

The next morning, before she opened the coffee shop, she walked to Logan's Crossing. As the sun rose, she walked up and down the boulevard of shops. There was no Whisker & Claw shop. As the stores opened, she caught the managers. They all had shaken their heads at the company name. When she described her brother, her factual description was lost on most of the managers until she mentioned his swollen eye.

"Yeah, I remember him," a burger and hotdog vendor said. "He bought a dog from me a couple of days ago. Looked like he was having a bad day."

"Has he been back?" she asked.

The man shook his head sadly.

Becca stood on the sidewalk as cars sped by. The shops hustled and bustled and went about daily life as if it didn't matter that her brother was missing. That was when she began to get scared. Very scared.

"And you're sure that no one else saw him after that time you saw him on the sidewalk?" a police officer asked. The police wouldn't even see her until the fourth day. At her kitchen table, she slid a picture of Cyrus and a description of his clothes to him. She shook her head.

"And there's nowhere else you think he might be?" the officer asked. "Is there any reason to believe that he could be in Indiana or a surrounding state? Any friends and family out that way?"

She shook her head again.

"We'll start looking, but I have to tell you that this is a needle in a haystack, Miss Grant. He could be anywhere. We'll see if we can track his cell phone, but it may be best if you organize a search party as well."

The officer waited as Becca ripped off her bandanna and dabbed her eyes with it. "Miss Grant, was your brother in hard times before he left?"

Becca told him everything; about the breakup, about Cyrus sleepwalking through life, and how he just couldn't let Jules go.

"We handle a lot of missing persons," the officer said, "Miss Grant, did your brother ever express to you any thoughts of self-harm or suicide?"

And then she lost it, unable to compose herself for the rest of the interview.

The only thing she could think of after that point was her brother, lying face-down in the river. Every night, she dreamt the same dream, but in a different flavor. A phone call with the worst news. An email to her with a letter from him explaining why he did it. And every time, she woke up in a cold sweat in the middle of the night, car horns blaring outside, and headlights brushing against her window curtains.

Becca even had to resort to calling Jules.

"Jules, I'm so sorry to do this, but this is Becca Grant. Have you seen Cyrus?"

Jules wasn't happy to hear Becca's voice. "Why can't you just leave me alone?"

"I would. I have. And if it makes you feel any better, I've been all over him to let you go," Becca said. "But Cyrus has gone missing. He hasn't been home in four days, and the police are searching for him. I was wondering if he had come by your place at all."

Jules's voice, which had begun the phone call with anger

and annoyance, turned fragile, as if it were about to break. "No, not since he and my boyfriend got into a fight outside my house."

Becca said nothing. Why would God grant her a break now, of all times?

The hardest call had been to her mom. The third time. In less than an hour, Aurora bolted through the front doors of the Wicked Cat, and they held each other. In the middle of the afternoon rush. All her patrons fell away, and the only thing she could feel was the hole in her heart. Aurora mounted a search party that went to all of Cyrus's old haunts, but to no avail.

Becca couldn't bring herself to join. She was too scared of what she would find—nothing. Or worse. All she could do was drown herself in the day-to-day running of the coffee shop—bullshit things like what beans to order, the right time for coupons, and customer complaints about the porcelain cups that she loved so much but seemed to chip every single week. While making a latte one evening with a flower design, she messed up and had to remake it. Then she remembered that Cyrus, for all his failings, was a pretty good barista. He wouldn't have screwed it up. She broke down in the middle of the evening rush.

The months piled onto each other, every day less optimistic than the last.

The events of the last few months swirled around her and choked her as she chugged the beer.

Cristián entered the shop. "We walked most of the neighborhood again today," he said. He shook his head as he gave her the news. "Becca, why don't you take a few days off?" he asked. "You look like hell. You're not thinking right. I'll manage the shop for you. You don't even have to pay me extra. I'm worried about you."

Becca crumpled the can of beer and tossed it behind her. It bounced off a mirror and dribbled across the floor.

"I'm fine," she said, just like Cyrus had said to her.

Autopilot took over, and somehow she found her way outside, into the private entrance of her building, up the rickety wooden stairs, and into her apartment, where, to feel closer to Cyrus, she played Bee Gees songs all night.

CHAPTER SIXTEEN

Through Cyrus's rat eyes, distant shapes took form in the pear-colored world. He made out swaying, shadowed columns, but he couldn't be sure of what they were.

"It's all right," Murgalen said. "My ask is simple. Do this one thing for me and I will send you home so that you can be human again."

Cyrus floated, sniffing. He couldn't believe the words. He was a rat. Had he fainted when she told him?

He felt himself drifting downward. Warm air ran across his coarse hair, bristling it. Several whiskers protruding from his back beamed sensations to his brain.

Descending. Descending.

A frantic voice spoke in his head, cleaving his human thoughts.

Rise. Rise.

The voice was like a chipmunk's. It ran parallel to his current thoughts, but much louder. He found his body arching of its own accord. His claws stretched. The hair on his hump rose.

Suddenly, his claws seized on a hard, grainy surface with sharp ridges.

He was standing on something.

He stood on his hind legs and sniffed. His whiskers moved back-and-forth on his head like a constellation of wires. Each one had a mind of its own, and a personality.

A weird voice spoke inside his mind.

Tree memory. A tree. A safe tree.

No owls. Or falcons.

Shade. Need shade. Run.

He ran, his claws scratching the textured surface. He looked down at the gnarled surface, lips of bark that could cut a human hand. But it was so damned blurry, even though it was right in front of him. Instead, his nose did the talking. Was he in a tree?

Murgalen began to sing again.

The tree shifted, an explosion of leaves and cracking branches. Cyrus rose into the air and dug in with his claws as the tree oriented itself sideways. He clung to the bark, his heart racing.

Something electric brushed against his face. In an instant, his whiskers beamed the message to him of pulsing energy, like glowing chain links. The links buzzed and hummed.

Murgalen sang again. Her voice comforted him, and also drove him forward.

"Gnaw the chains, my loves."

Then she sang a wordless song, her voice rising and falling, floating around him, drifting away and back again like a boomerang. And all the while, the bark kept rising and falling.

He had the intense urge to gnaw. His incisors made their presence known, and he imagined something, anything against them to dull his stress and take his mind off of the maddening song.

He was upon the links instantly. And he finally got a blurred look at interlocking links that kept rustling as the bark rose and fell.

He gnawed at a spot flush with energy, ground his incisors

on it a few times. Numbness washed across his mouth. God, this felt good.

But not good enough.

He moved along the links, testing them, gnawing at points. His whiskers swept tirelessly over the links, telling him to keep going. Every so often, the chain zapped him, making him jump and his hairs stand on end.

His rat brain spoke to him frantically.

Weakness. Weakness ahead.

Feels good.

Another.

He sniffed the air. A rank odor of sweat drifted into his nostrils. And then the smell of piss screamed to his brain.

Death. Death. Death!

Heart stopped.

Stop!

Stop!!

He sniffed, unsure how to process the message. The scent of the urine passed somewhat and he kept running until his whiskers seized on a suitable spot ahead.

And then his incisors were in the energy chain again, gnawing a half-bitten link. His teeth filed against the energy, a constant buzzing in his skull. All the while, Murgalen continued her beautiful song, and the bark rose up and down and the chains rustled in a metallic harmony and the stench of death wafted up from below in waves that smelled like a song of its own.

He chomped another link and it zapped him again—this time so hard, it knocked him into the green sky. He stretched out his legs. His tail sprang up behind him, a twirling propeller behind him as his eyes widened.

He smashed into the dirt and bounced several times before rolling to a stop.

The stench of death smothered him.

His whiskers lit up a trail toward a dark mass inches away.

A dead rat, lying on its back, feet curled upon its body, stared at the sky.

Cyrus squeaked and jumped backward.

Another rat lay dead.

His heart pounded in his chest as smell after smell bombarded him and his whiskers kept beaming thoughts to him.

Rat. Rat. Rat. Days old dead. Weeks old dead. Electrocuted. Carcasses with no skin on the bone.

He was standing in a field of dead rats.

But not rats.

A familiar smell came to him, one he knew from his earliest memories—the lingering scent of human skin. He smelled it as an undertone in the puddles of piss scattered across the endless landscape. It put his rat brain on alert.

The human scent.

He wasn't surrounded by rats.

He was surrounded by humans.

CHAPTER SEVENTEEN

Zane Brooks couldn't process his transformation. It struck him as a joke. A high-end, multimillion-dollar joke by a so-called doctor waiting in the wings with cameramen to document the experience.

At least, that was what he thought until he lost his vision. Panic set in, and he clawed at the space around him trying to get hold of something.

What was this place? He had ended up in a dull green world before suddenly transforming into this...this monstrosity.

His claws grasped air. He floated, suffocating in this place, not knowing up from down.

All he wanted now was to go back home. Back to the crappy, collapsing apartment. He would have done anything to get his old self back.

He thought of Thurston and seethed. That fucking doctor did this to him.

Out of nowhere, a soft voice spoke to him.

"Zane, don't be afraid."

The woman's voice pulled him from his thoughts.

Her voice soothed him.

"You are a rat now," she said.

Zane's curse words came out as shrill squeaks. He landed on a surface of tree bark.

"Help me," she said. "And I will set you free."

Zane sniffed a buzzing chain of magical energy.

"I will send you to the man who did this," she said. "I will send you to Thurston."

Hearing the doctor's name enraged him and he sank his teeth into the magic, twisting as his jaws closed.

A heady scent drifted to him from below. A woman's scent.

"Chew, my love," she said. "And you'll have your time for revenge."

As Zane chewed through the chain, the woman began to sing again.

CHAPTER EIGHTEEN

A TREE BRANCH scooped Cyrus up and carried him through the pear darkness. Though he couldn't see, he sensed the presence of other rats along the giant structure.

Were they Zane, Henry, and Jenae? He didn't know why, but in some strange, sick, and twisted way, he knew they were with him in this place.

The branch deposited him on the surface he had been on before.

He got to work again, gnawing in rhythm with Murgalen's song. It calmed him amidst the uncertainty, and the only thing he could think of was digging his incisors into weaknesses in the magic. The links weren't hard; just stubborn, zapping him every now and again. And every time he ripped a hole in it, the intoxicating scent of human skin spiraled into his nose. He couldn't stop chewing, couldn't stop sniffing the scent of the bark just below the magical energy.

In the distance, he heard the others doing the same. Murgalen's song seemed to grow happier, more high-pitched.

He settled into the same rhythm. His whiskers told him where to bite, and he did; tore out chunks of magic and sniffed with delight. Soon, something shattered, and the magical energy zoomed away.

His whiskers rubbed across a mixture of bark and skin. Soft, supple skin that took him back to a memory.

The time when he and Jules had been fooling around in her apartment. What started as a back-and-forth of awkward kisses progressed to close on the floor and lying in each other's arms on a noisy futon that she had bought from Goodwill. His hands explored every part of her body, and hers did his. And suddenly, she took him into her mouth and he closed his eyes with pleasure and pain, brushing his hands against her cheek. And then he was inside her and they were moving together as one on the futon that creaked and creaked. Her skin on his, electric and new. He didn't care so much about the sensations as he did exploring her.

That was what his whiskers sensed right now. Skin. Bark. Electricity. Something moist moved next to him. Inching closer, he stared at a giant eyeball that moved around quickly in its socket. It locked on him.

He was on Murgalen's cheek.

"My dear Cyrus," she said. "How good it is to see you."

She sang a new song now, and Cyrus felt her head rising ever upward. Something squeaked below. The other rats—they were falling.

"Don't worry about them," she said.

A giant hand of half bark, half skin dug into the bark around the other eye and, with a powerful rip, a giant square went flying, destroying the last of the magic. Her fingers grabbed remnants of the chains and heaved them away.

She wasn't a woman, even though she was half skin and half bark. Her teeth and jaw were one; ragged triangles of gnarled bark. Strands of red hair were matted on her head, with a crown of dagger-sharp branches. Her eyes, green at first glance, were pixelated forests of tree canopies.

Her song echoed throughout the soupy world. She plucked

Cyrus off her cheek and into a rough palm, bringing him to her face.

"I will never forget what you have done for me," she said, smiling. "Our race will never forget you, Cyrus."

Cyrus squeaked in fright.

"They can't hold me in my land," Murgalen said. "Those fools will regret the day they bound me with magic!"

Murgalen shook herself free of more bark, which sloughed off of her and crashed to the ground, covering many of the dead rats. Only then did he realize how massive and thick she truly was. But before he could squeak at her, Murgalen pulled her lips into a blow, and a warm thermal flipped Cyrus through the air and out of the world of the fae.

He woke up in the sewer drain, covered in tree bark. The drain, just like before, was bathed in complete darkness. His rat eyes adjusted somewhat, and he stood, yawning.

He wasn't alone. Another rat lay next to him, waking up. Two others lay further down the drain.

Cyrus took several steps back from the other rats. The rat next to him hissed, its hair standing on end.

On instinct, Cyrus hissed back.

The other rat gave no warning; it was upon him, claws bared. They grasped each other, pulling each other onto their hind legs, screaming violently.

A male voice called their names.

"Cyrus, Zane, stop!"

Henry was in his human form, on his knees in the drain. Though it was pitch black, Cyrus knew his breathing.

Zane? Was the rat boxing him right now with its incisors bared *Zane*?

Cyrus let go and he and the other rat fell to their feet.

He didn't know why, but an urge surged through him, a

new possibility—the possibility to become something else. He focused on the thought and found his body lengthening, his incisors shrinking, his tail receding into his back, and his hair stretching out and inverting itself into skin. His bones plucked and popped into human form, and he ignored the pain as much as he could. His clothes were heavier on him now, soaking wet with mud and filth.

Seconds later, he and Zane were on all fours, panting and staring at each other. With his human eyes, he could only make out a faint outline of the beefy man.

"Cyrus?" Zane asked.

"It's me," he said.

Jenae spoke as well. "Looks like we're all safe."

"Define safe," Zane said, coughing.

"It's cold," Henry said. "I don't know what happened to my flashlight."

"Same here," Cyrus said.

"We need to find the hole we fell from," Jenae said. "That's the only way we'll get out."

They fumbled around in the darkness, and no light source betrayed the drain covering's location.

"I can't see anything," Zane said. "Goddamn if we don't rot down here."

They sat, mud and trickles of water running against them. Somewhere, water dripped.

"What we saw," Cyrus said, "did you—"

"The tree woman?" Henry asked. "We didn't fucking imagine it, if that's what you're asking."

"What did she do to us?" Jenae asked, pain and hurt in her voice. "She—she—"

"Turned us into rats," Zane said. "Her and that doctor bastard."

"But why?" Cyrus asked. "What did Murgalen tell all of you?"

"Tell?" Henry asked. "She didn't tell me anything except for good luck."

"She told me that I was lucky to be spared," Jenae said. "Oh, and thank you."

"That right?" Zane asked. "Well, she told me that the good doctor was responsible for all of this."

"She didn't even tell us her name," Jenae said.

"Nope," Zane said.

"What about you, Cyrus?" Henry asked.

Cyrus remembered his conversation with Murgalen. He had been the only one she gave her name to. And she had told him so much else. But why not the others? She definitely didn't mention Thurston.

"She just sang," Cyrus lied.

"I thought so," Zane said.

"I have an idea," Cyrus said, wanting to change subjects. "We're humans again. But can we turn back into rats?"

"Why?" Jenae asked. "That was the most disgusting feeling I've ever experienced."

"I don't know about the rest of you," Cyrus said, "but my rat senses were insane. I couldn't see much, but all my other senses made up for it. Maybe we can use those to find a way out."

"That's some good thinkin'," Zane said. "I knew I liked you, kid."

Cyrus stood and went first. He remembered the sensation of being a rat, and the memories of the faerie world. His body shrank, and in seconds, he was splashing around in the water as his rat self.

Soon, Zane, Henry, and Jenae were splashing around with him.

The transformation into a rat made the drain even darker. Cyrus was completely blind now. Zane squeaked and charged ahead.

Cyrus's rat instinct took over and he found himself against

the wall. The sensation of touching the cold surface brought him comfort as he smeared his cheeks on the bricks. His whiskers pushed forward, tasting the brick, and the wet, rough texture kept him against it.

Cyrus followed Zane, and as a train, they made their way down the drain in stops and starts. Every few feet, they stopped to sense the environment. Mostly it was all the same except for universes of smells they moved into here and there.

Cyrus detected an opening just ahead. Zane must have detected it too because he raced ahead without stopping.

The tunnel opened at the top into a long, narrow shaft.

The shaft where they had entered.

A few seconds later, they were human, craning their necks to get a better view of it.

"This is it," Zane said. "Good idea, Cyrus."

"It's a long way up," Jenae said. "Especially in the dark."

"We'll have to boost each other," Henry said. "Zane, can you climb up and let us use you as a ladder?"

"Sure thing, boss," he said. "All them weight-lifting sessions are gonna pay off."

He was silent.

"But first, there's something we gotta talk about," Zane said. "The way I figure, the lady turned us into rats, but it was the doctor that fed us to her. He's gotta be up there. And if he is, he dies."

Cyrus gulped.

"He's gotta pay for what he's done," Zane said. "All that shit he told us about trying to find rats—it was all lies. We're never gonna be the same again. We're rats, for Christ's sake. No telling what kind of long-lasting impact this'll have."

"We can't murder him," Cyrus said. "That's...illegal."

"Oh, so turning people into rats doesn't deserve punishment, eh, Cyrus?" Zane asked harshly. "This ain't the time to take the moral high road. When we get up there, the doctor gets it."

"But, Zane—"

"Did you see all the dead rat people on the ground?" Zane asked. "You want him to turn more people like us into rats and kill them?"

"No, but—"

"Then he dies," Zane said. "And if none of you want to help me, I'll strangle him myself, with my bare hands."

It was a while before Henry spoke up. "Zane's right. No one is going to help us."

"But what I don't understand is why," Cyrus said. "*Why* did he do this to us? It doesn't make sense. If we knew why, maybe we could—"

"It don't matter why," Zane said. "All that matters is that we stop the psychopath."

Silence.

"You got a problem with that?" Zane asked.

"I'm not killing anyone," Cyrus said. "I'm not a murderer. There has to be another way."

"Then that makes you a witness to what I'm about to do," Zane said. "If you don't come along, Cyrus, you're gonna regret it."

A sharp wave of fear spread through Cyrus's body as Zane approached him.

"Back off," he said, retreating.

"I'll back off when you agree to the plan," Zane said. "Henry's on board. What about you, Jenae?"

After a pause, Jenae said "This is up to us, Cyrus."

Cyrus shook his head, even though no one could see him.

"What'll it be?" Zane asked.

"No," Cyrus said.

Out of nowhere, Zane tackled him, and they fell into the mud. Henry and Jenae yelled and told them to stop.

"Whether you like it or not, we're a team," Zane said. "We do this together."

"Get off me!"

Cyrus deflected a hand racing toward his eye. But Zane was too strong.

Then, he got the idea to become a rat. His body shrank out of Zane's reach. He jumped up and bit Zane on the ankle.

"You want to settle this Mother Nature style, then!" Zane said, shrinking.

They circled each other as rats, not seeing but sensing each other.

Zane squeaked.

Cyrus squeaked back.

In an instant, Zane was upon him, but Cyrus darted to the side, keeping his face toward Zane.

Zane bared his incisors and hissed.

Cyrus waited, his hairs raised, all senses on alert.

Predictably, Zane rushed him, but Cyrus was ready and jumped out of the way just as Zane gnashed his teeth, narrowly missing Cyrus's tail.

Zane charged again and they rose to their hind legs, boxing and grappling, nipping at each other's faces—not to kill, but to wound.

But they were both too fast for each other, their whiskers mixing and betraying the other's location.

Zane punched Cyrus gently on the chest.

They backed off, both landing on all fours.

Cyrus's heart raced.

Though they had never fought before, they were playing a game that had ancestral rules. Cyrus listened as his rat brain told him the rules.

Bite his rump. Bite his rump. Don't let him bite yours.

Zane dashed at him, and Cyrus circled out of the way again, but Zane anticipated it and head-butted Cyrus in the side, knocking him at the wall.

Cyrus slashed a claw at Zane as he approached, scoring him across the face.

Zane hissed and charged, knocking Cyrus against the wall.

Just as quickly as it started, it was over—Zane's incisors buried into Cyrus's hairy rump.

Cyrus squeaked in pain and Zane let go, backing away.

The two rats stood, huffing.

Even though he had so much more energy left...even though he could have fought to the death, a primal impulse told Cyrus to stop fighting. That he had lost.

Zane transformed back into a human, his ugly face leering at Cyrus.

"I win. Let's go. You get the honor of going up first."

Cyrus wasn't going to be a murderer. No matter what happened, he wasn't going to jail!

He dashed down the sewer, away from the group.

"Get back here!" Zane yelled.

Cyrus ran as fast as his little feet could carry him.

Soon Zane was behind him in rat form, racing after him. The few seconds' head start made it difficult to catch up.

His whiskers waved left and steered toward the wall, into another drain. This one was smaller and barely big enough for even his rat body.

The water was deeper here.

He turned into another opening. Rushing water gargled in the distance, along with a sound like fingers typing furiously on a typewriter.

He crashed into the moving herd of insects before his whiskers caught up with the image. Hundreds of finger-sized cockroaches crawled on the walls of the drain—no, the walls themselves were moving, their antennae wavering and their legs clicking against the brick.

Cyrus's human voice screamed inside his head as he plowed through dozens of roaches. They crunched under his claws, and they were a little too close for comfort since his rat body was so low to the ground.

The cockroaches didn't faze Zane. He was gaining ground.

Cyrus smelled water mixed with garbage and mud.

His whiskers warned him to stop, and he did, just on the edge of a drop-off into a flowing drain full of sewage, human waste, and storm water. Though he couldn't see the current, it was strong, spraying a fine mist on his face.

WHAM!

Zane barreled into him from behind and he somersaulted through the air. The last thing he saw before he hit the water was Zane's blurry rat face. Had he been smirking?

Cyrus squeaked before he went under, and the current pulled him deep into the city sewer system.

———

CHAPTER NINETEEN

———

IN HUMAN FORM, Zane returned to the hole where Henry and Jenae were waiting.

"Where's Cyrus?" Jenae asked.

"He fell into a sewer stream," Zane said. "The current took him. I have no idea where he is right now, but it would be a miracle if he survives."

In the dim light, Henry and Jenae looked at each other sadly.

"Don't mourn for him!" Zane barked. "We are all in agreement. He wasn't. It's a good thing he's gone."

It took him several tries to jump onto the bottom step of the well, but he caught the rusty step and hung on as tightly as he could while Jenae and Henry used his body to raise themselves onto the metal steps. Once they were all safely on the ladder, they shifted into rats, climbing nimbly over the spot where the steps had sheared from the wall, and up into the floor of the Damen Silos basement.

Jenae climbed over first. She let out a small squeak.

Then Henry jumped over.

As if showing off, Zane flipped out of the sewer and landed on his feet. But not on cement like he expected.

His feet were stuck in glue. He tried to move a foot, but it was attached to an off-white card with a picture of a rat on it.

Zane squeaked in fright when he saw Jenae and Henry also stuck in glue traps, trying to free their feet, but just as thoroughly glued to the paper.

The entire perimeter around the drain opening was covered in glue traps.

Zane's first instinct was to turn back into a human, but a metallic click stopped him from transforming.

Thurston stood over them with a revolver.

"Well, well," he said, "if I didn't catch some rats."

He knelt, with the revolver pointed directly in front of Zane's face. "I'm going to ask you some questions, and you are going to answer. One squeak means yes. Two squeaks means no. You lie, you die, got it?"

The rats said nothing.

"Did you free her?" the doctor asked.

Henry squeaked.

Though the doctor's face was blurry, Zane could never mistake a smile; an impish, mischievous smile.

"Did she come with you? Is she down there?"

Jenae squeaked twice.

Anger replaced his smile.

"Which one of you is missing? Zane?"

They squeaked twice.

"Henry?"

They squeaked twice.

"Jenae?"

They squeaked twice.

"Is Cyrus down there?"

The rats were silent.

"Is Cyrus down there?" the doctor asked, booming.

Zane gulped.

Jenae was first. She squeaked twice. Henry squeaked with her. Twice.

The doctor pointed the revolver at Zane. "Well?"

Zane gulped again. He squeaked once.

"Which is it?" the doctor asked. "Who wants to die first?"

Jenae lay on her bed of glue. She squeaked twice.

Henry squeaked twice.

The doctor's face loomed big in front of Zane. "They're lying, aren't they?"

Henry and Jenae squabbled, protesting. Their shrieks hurt Zane's ears.

"Either I've got a dead rat or a renegade on my hands," the doctor said. "And none of you got me results. If you freed her, why isn't she here?"

Thurston stood. Henry and Jenae were the first to go. The bullets blew their bodies across the room like wind carrying sheets of paper.

Zane shrieked for mercy in the last few seconds of his life, but the bullet ripped through him all the same, knocking his body into the drain.

The gunsmoke swept around Thurston as he dropped the revolver and fell to his knees.

"No, no, no..."

It had been three months since Murgalen spoke to him, until just a few hours ago, when the boutonnière came alive again and she warned him to get back to the silos. Three months since she promised that they would finally be together. She left him to pace, to stew in his thoughts. What was a man to do with himself if he couldn't speak to the woman he loved?

But the rats said they freed her. Could it have been true? Did something happen to her? He beat his hands against his head, crying out in pain and love sickness.

And then, the boutonnière came alive and spoke.

"My love, why so angry?"

Thunder growled outside. Thurston looked the window of the basement where storm clouds washed out the landscape outside, watching as if he were staring at the face of God.

"I am alive, and I am well," Murgalen said. "And we will be together soon, Atty."

"I must see you," he said. "Now that you're free, we—"

"I am preparing for my return," Murgalen said.

"There's one last thing," Thurston said. "Cyrus lives."

"I will allow it," Murgalen said.

"I won't," Thurston said.

"Why is that, Atty?"

"Our love will die in secret," Thurston said. "As long as he lives, he'll talk. And the other paranormals will find us. I intend to keep you all to myself."

Murgalen took a few seconds to speak.

"You're sure about this, Atty?" Murgalen asked. "That he's alive?"

"The whole point of this plan was no survivors," Thurston said.

"Very well, my love."

Thurston turned giddy. "By God, I did it. I really did it. I'm so close."

"You did, but you're not done yet, are you?"

"No."

Thurston rose. He took the bloodied carcasses of the rats, tossed them into the drain, replaced the cover, and with a shovel, dumped a mound of dirt onto it. He cast the shovel aside and climbed out of the basement through the same ragged maw in which he'd entered.

It was raining. A violent storm. Thunder shook the ground and lightning lashed the sky, veining spectacular forks over the Chicago skyline. Thurston opened his umbrella, walked to the front gate where the security guard sat in his white pickup, tipped his Cubs hat to him, and started down the long, quiet road to the L station.

He seemed to recall that Cyrus had given an address on his paperwork. Somewhere in Logan Square.

CHAPTER TWENTY

Cyrus knelt on the gravel beach, hardly able to walk.

He recalled his voyage through the sewer current—through refuse, human waste, and storm water until it spat him out into the Chicago River. The last remnants of rain lingered in the air from the storm that had washed him through the city drains.

The storm clouds were clearing from the navy sky, and the lights of the city blurred against Cyrus's vision like bokeh in an unfocused camera lens.

He was covered in his garbage and filth, back in human form, lying next to his own vomit. He rolled over, cheek smacking against gravel. The river turned sideways and he gasped for air. Summoning a cluster of energy deep within, he transformed himself into a rat.

He stumbled across the gravel, unable to see but relying on his whiskers and sense of smell to propel him forward.

He had to get to safety. But where could he go?

A giant shadow covered him and descended from the sky. Alarms sounded in his head and his body went into high alert, but it was too late.

Two claws seized his back and pulled him into the air.

Cyrus shrieked as the gravel beach and the Chicago River and the roads below grew smaller.

A familiar gronk made him look up.

It was a raven. The beautiful raven he had seen earlier, with the blue-tinged wings. It was carrying him high into the sky.

The other raven flapped next to them, gronking at Cyrus.

The last thing Cyrus remembered was seeing the city skyline go diagonal as the ravens turned and flew toward it.

CHAPTER TWENTY-ONE

"Special delivery for Miss Becca Grant."

Becca excused herself from the evening rush to meet a flower boy at the front door. A kid no older than eighteen held the biggest bouquet that she had ever seen. The flowers covered his face, and he had to stick his neck around it to see her.

"For me?" she asked. "I think you've got the wrong place, kid."

"Becca Grant?" the boy asked.

She accepted the flowers. "I wasn't expecting these."

The boy handed her a card. She opened it with one hand. A message was printed on it in computerized cursive handwriting: "We love what you're doing with the Wicked Cat. Keep being a model for Chicago. Yours truly, The Coffee Roasters Association of America."

Becca read the message with skepticism. Sure, she was doing a great job, but why flowers?

"Do you have a name of a person who sent this?" she asked.

The boy shook his head. "We're not able to share that, ma'am. Have a great day."

The door chime rang as the boy pushed out of the store onto the rain-slicked streets, hopped onto a bicycle, and pedaled away.

Becca sniffed, taking in an intoxication of red roses, white carnations, purple daisies, and floral mist. The flowers took her back to her childhood when Mom used to buy flowers every week and put them on the dining room table, just because.

"So you *do* have a boyfriend," Cristián said. "Why do you lead me on?"

"Not a boyfriend," Becca said sternly. "A…professional admirer."

"A professional lover?" Cristián asked, smirking. "Do tell."

"The honest answer is I've never heard of these people before," she said, glancing at the card again.

She excused herself and took the flowers up to her apartment. She set them on the dining room table, reveling again in the spring aroma that filled the room. Hadn't she needed flowers these last few days? Maybe that was what was missing, other than her brother.

She made a mental note to look up the Coffee Roasters Association of America when she got off work.

Thurston sat on a park bench across from the coffee shop, sipping a to-go cup from the Wicked Cat.

The apartment light above the shop blinked on for a minute or so, then blinked off. Shortly after, Becca exited the private entrance and dipped into the shop, taking her place behind the counter again.

He watched her for a few minutes, studying her tomboyish mannerisms. She looked like Cyrus. Even had some of his mannerisms. It'd be a shame if she had to perish along with him.

He finished the last of his coffee and walked away, wondering what the Coffee Roasters Association of America would truly think of the Wicked Cat, if it existed.

CHAPTER TWENTY-TWO

Cyrus woke up on a bed of cedar shavings. The soft bedding was as comfortable as a mattress to his rat body, and he turned over a few times, smelling the clean scent that reminded him of his uncle's farm in central Illinois. The white barn with the quarter horses, the mountains of shavings, and Timothy hay…

He scratched an itch on his face and yawned. He stretched his legs, bending down and sticking his hump and tail into the air.

Where was he?

It was late. Middle of the night.

Several shadows lay in the distance. A wooden post. Paint. On the walls. A chest full of freshly laundered clothes. Divinely feminine. A closet full of shoes. Leather. Lots and lots of leather.

In the next room, the aroma of coffee, completely black… and…pizza? Pepperoni!

Cyrus stood on the cedar shavings, taking in the symphony of smells. Underneath it all, the undertone of flesh—a woman's *and* a man's, scents like dueling dragons, constantly trying to one-up each other in his nostrils.

Then he noticed the sound of running water against tile. A shower. The water shut off. A man whistled, and Cyrus heard the abrasive sound of a towel scraping across wet skin, a sensation that made his hair stand on end.

The earth quaked and Cyrus hid in the corner of the box.

The smell of wintergreen and rubber preceded a man entering the room, barefoot and in nothing but a brown towel. He was gigantic compared to Cyrus's rat body, and prey instinct set in. Cyrus nestled himself as far into the corner of the box as he could.

The man bent down, his face coming into hazy view.

Cyrus recognized him.

Rocco. From the Wicked Cat. The guy that was...hitting on him.

"You're awake," Rocco said, smiling. "About time, bud. We thought you were toast."

Cyrus squeaked.

"You don't have to stay a rat," Rocco said. "You're safe here."

Cyrus hopped out of the box and grew into his human form, on his knees. The soft gray carpet was a miracle compared to the surfaces he'd been walking on lately.

Rocco's face sharpened into high definition. He was still dripping from the shower, his hair a soppy mess. Water glistened on his chest, which looked like something off the cover of an erotica novel.

"Whew," Rocco said. "You are foul."

Cyrus got a look around. He was in a bedroom. A giant white four-poster bed dominated half the room. A lamp on a nightstand was turned down low. The sheets were pink.

A shadow slipped around Rocco, and Luna joined him. She was wearing a pink flannel shirt with a white undershirt that cut off at her midriff. She put her hands on her hips and clicked her tongue at Cyrus.

"You owe me the cost of a carpet cleaning," she said.

Cyrus glanced at the floor. The carpet under him was black and green from the wastewater dripping off his clothes.

"Sorry," he said. Then he paused, looking at the couple again. "You're the ravens."

"Congratulations, Captain Obvious," Luna said. "We picked you up some clothes because we figured you'd need them. Sorry in advance if they're not a perfect fit. We got you some pizza too. Why don't you shower first?"

Luna pointed to a stack of clothes folded neatly on her bed: jeans, a white t-shirt, underwear, socks, and a pair of black skateboard shoes.

"We'll tell you everything once you're comfortable," Rocco said.

"And why don't *you* get dressed too?" Luna asked, walking away and dragging a finger across his shoulder.

Rocco laughed. "Right. Guess this is a little weird, isn't it, bud?"

Cyrus found his way to Luna's bathroom, undressed, climbed into the shower, and turned on the hot water. Her bathroom was like a typical old Chicago apartment: super tiny with god-awful tile colors in the shower. Luna's shower was black and green.

He stood under the water with his head down, thinking about Thurston, Murgalen, and Zane. And the ravens...who were they, really? How did they find him?

He rinsed himself with Rocco's minty body wash and stood in the water until it ran cold and stung his skin. After toweling off, he nuked the shower in bleach that Luna left out, and scrubbed with a sponge until his hands hurt. He put his clothes in a trash bag.

"Sausage or pepperoni?" Rocco asked, holding up a plate of deep-dish pizza as Cyrus walked into Luna's small living room. Rocco had slipped into a t-shirt that accentuated his pecks. The picturesque, cake-like slice in his hand dripped with cheese. Cyrus's stomach rumbled.

"Pepperoni is the *only* choice," he said, settling at the table.

Rocco slid him a plate of pepperoni pizza and a can of strawberry soda. Cyrus dug in as if it were the Last Supper. Only after a few bites did he look around at Luna's small apartment. Hardwood floors, no view except the roof of the next building and an alley, an air conditioner on the wall, and two lonely couches, one on which Luna sat barefoot, singing along to a song on the radio, nursing a glass of wine.

"So…who are you guys?" Cyrus asked after he engulfed the pizza slice.

Luna switched off the radio.

"You kind of gave off strange vibes back in the coffee shop," Cyrus said, cracking open the can of strawberry soda.

"That's the paranormal essence," Rocco said. "When people come into contact with it, they don't know how to respond."

"My friend said you were hitting on me," Cyrus said. "Thought you wanted me for a ménage à trois."

Luna choked on her wine and laughed. Rocco was shocked at her outburst at first then laughed along with her. "What happens in the sack is our business," he said. "But maybe we ought to work on our first impressions next time, eh, babe?"

"When someone's life is on the line, we don't think about first impressions," Luna said. "And the fact that we couldn't convince you saddened us, Cyrus."

"You talked to me on the street at the Logan's Crossing shops," Cyrus said. "As ravens."

"That clue was about as obvious as it should've gotten," Luna said. "What part of the words 'doctor' and 'regret' did you not understand?"

"We don't usually like to make calls in person," Rocco said. "It can get the Regulators pissed off at us. But we were willing to do it for you because we knew how much danger you were in. But even then, there was only so much we could say."

"How can you turn into ravens?" Cyrus asked.

"We are shifters," Rocco said. "Much like you can turn into a rat, we can turn into ravens just by thinking about it. We're paranormals."

"Paranormal? Like ghosts?" Cyrus asked.

"We're not ghosts," Luna said. She joined them at the table. "We were born as shifters. Sometime around age twenty, we discovered that we were able to shift. That's right around the age most shifters realize their power. You, on the other hand, are one unusual dude."

"Wait, so Thurston didn't transform you into animals?" Cyrus asked, scratching his head.

"We're not lab rats, if that's what you're suggesting," Luna said. "No offense. We're natural-born shifters."

"As ravens, we see things that the normal world can't," Rocco said. "A raven can sense dying animals. It's why they're so good at finding food. But as shifters, we can also sense dying souls. And this city is full of them."

"And on the day we met you, we knew your soul was lost," Luna said. "We just didn't know how long you had."

"But I don't understand," Cyrus said. "How did you know about the doctor?"

"We've been aware of him for some time," Rocco said. "He's been abducting innocent people. You're the first person we know of who has interacted with Thurston and come back alive. We thought you were a goner. When I patted you on the shoulder that night at the Wicked Cat, I put a tracking spell on you. Your essence disappeared from the world the next day, and Luna and I thought you were gone forever. Then you reappeared on that beach. We were lucky to have found you in time. We never found the others before they died."

"Others?" Cyrus asked.

"You're the only living rat shifter we've been able to find,"

Rocco said. "Now maybe *you* can tell us what the hell is going on."

"So you're telling me that my soul was dying?" Cyrus asked.

"In a sense," Luna said. "Normal humans go about their business, and they never think twice about the paranormal world around them because they can't see it. That's by design. But occasionally, the two worlds do come into contact with each other, and humans are the ones who pay for it—sometimes with their lives."

"This is crazy," Cyrus said.

"You were an unlucky casualty," Rocco said. "We're sorry that this happened to you."

Cyrus pushed away from the table and paced the living room. "If I was in danger, why didn't you just tell me the truth at the coffee shop? Why did you have to be so cryptic?"

"As paranormals, we are forbidden from revealing the supernatural world to a human unless they are in imminent danger," Luna said. "It's an unwritten rule among us. Like I said, we are so sorry, Cyrus."

"Um, I *was* in mortal danger," Cyrus said. "And now I'm a rat."

"Rat shifter," Rocco corrected. "If you were a wererat, we would be having a completely different conversation."

"The only exception we know of," Luna said, "would be, for example, if you were walking home from the L at night and got ambushed by a vampire. Unfortunately, that happens more often than you think. But a more elaborate plot to drag a human into the supernatural world? That's where it gets iffy, and where we can get into a lot of trouble if we break the rules."

Rocco put his hand on Cyrus's shoulder. "Someone's gotta tell you this, and someone's gotta tell it to you straight," he said. "Cyrus, your life will never be the same. It has changed in ways that you can't comprehend yet. I wish that we could wave a magic wand and turn you back into a human and make you forget all of this, but you're one of us now."

"Not exactly," Luna said. "But kind of."

"What do you mean *kind of?*" Cyrus asked.

"For starters, I don't know any shifter that was created," Luna said. "Shifters are born, not made. You're an anomaly. Second, I don't know any rat shifters. That honor belongs solely to you. And the fact that strange magic created your condition means that the Regulators are going to want to keep a close eye on you."

"Who are the Regulators?"

Someone knocked at the door. Rocco checked the peephole, undid the deadbolt, and opened the door.

A middle-aged black man in a Kangol beret, black silk shirt, and gold chain entered. He wore a neatly trimmed mustache and skinny beard streaked with gray, and his aura telegraphed "no-nonsense." He patted Rocco on the shoulder with a fraternal nod. Then he stopped in the kitchen, studied Cyrus for a moment, and said, "Cyrus Grant, it's not your fault, but you just screwed up the paranormal world something awful."

CHAPTER TWENTY-THREE

"Did I tear a hole in the time-space continuum?" Cyrus asked.

The black man stared at him, puzzled. "No."

Cyrus shrugged. "Then I guess the night could be worse."

Rocco and Luna busted into laughter.

Luna touched his arm. "That's exactly how you should take this. Bitter pill with laughter."

"This is Desmond Lovelace," Rocco said.

"I'm the captain of the Chicago precinct of the Regulators," Desmond finished. "It's nice to meet you, Mr. Grant, though I wish we didn't have to meet at all."

"We already broke the news to him, Des," Rocco said. "You know, the thing about life never being the same, and yada yada yada."

Desmond sat at the table. "Well, we might as well lay it on you, Mr. Grant. The Regulators are an organization dedicated to protecting humans from the paranormal world and helping unlucky humans cope with the consequences of paranormal interaction. We regulate the existence of paranormals in the city. Rocco and Luna are part of our shifter force. They're a warning system of sorts, using their animal senses to help us spot problems before they become tragedies. Everything we do, we do *without* tipping off the existence of the paranormal whenever possible. Many times, we're able to warn humans that they're walking into a trap and gently redirect them down another path where they won't be harmed. In your case, we failed. For people like you, we provide support services and mentorships to help ease the transition into the supernatural, because it's a bitch, Mr. Grant."

"A bitch is an understatement," Cyrus said. "Why couldn't you just TELL me what was going to happen instead of being cryptic? I don't buy the 'we can't save you because you're not in imminent danger' bullshit."

Desmond sighed. "If the entire world knew what really went bump in the night, Mr. Grant, it would tear itself apart with fear and paranoia. A lot of people would die. It would take the term 'witch hunt' to another level. Considering that many paranormals live and work alongside humans, it wouldn't be very smart to tip our existence to regular folks, would it? We have a vested interest in staying in the shadows, even though some of us may hate each other—and humans. The Regulators are a coalition of many different paranormal beings that exists to punish lawbreakers and clean up the messes they make in their wake."

Desmond stared at Cyrus searchingly. The guy was reading him. Cyrus tried not to show any emotion.

"Now that I've scared the bejesus out of you, it's your turn to scare us," Desmond said. "Do you mind telling us what happened to you?"

The guy was dead serious. He didn't look like the kind that smiled often. Was he a raven? If human personalities were an indicator of shifter animal type, then he definitely wasn't a raven. But then again, what was a *rat's* personality like?

"Don't you guys know what happened to me?" Cyrus asked. "I'm a sewer rat."

"We only saw bits and pieces from the outside from

following you," Desmond said. "We need to know what Thurston is up to so we can stop him. Start from the beginning, Mr. Grant."

Cyrus told them everything, from his meeting with Thurston to his fight with Zane and his death-defying surf through the sewers. Desmond listened intently, writing a few things down on a notepad that he produced from his pocket. Luna listened as if enraptured, her face mirroring the different feelings he went through—he noted that she was easy to read. Rocco listened with his arms folded.

"And the woman you spoke to," Desmond said. "What did she say her name was?"

"Murgalen," Cyrus said. "No idea how to spell that."

Desmond, Luna, and Rocco looked at each other.

"That's the missing link," Luna said. "Now we finally know who's behind this."

"She said she was a fae," Cyrus said. "Like a fairy, but different."

"Fae are magical beings who inhabit nature," Desmond said. "And they're quite a varied and diverse group. Murgalen is a nymph, also known as a Lesser Fae. They inhabit the natural aspects of the city—trees mainly, but water too. There are mountain nymphs out west. With the city's development, many of them have been losing power over the centuries. We've even heard accounts of nymphs dying after major construction projects."

"Nymphs are usually harmless," Rocco said. "There's only one way to set them off, and that's to disrespect nature."

"In those cases, we don't get involved," Desmond said. "It's perfectly fine for a paranormal to act in their own survival interests."

"If you're accusing me of destroying the environment, I've never done that," Cyrus said. "I mean, I've thrown some trash on the ground here and there, but—"

"We're not casting stones, Mr. Grant," Desmond said. "You didn't set Murgalen off. Thurston did."

"The guy used to be a famous researcher," Rocco said. "World expert in rats, apparently."

"Yeah, he definitely had a thing for rats," Cyrus said. "It was creepy."

"He was at the forefront of the research that underpinned the city's War on Rats," Desmond said. "By all accounts, he was a passionate guy. Sometimes a little too passionate. Word got out from a news report that his experiments were crossing ethical boundaries. Pissed a lot of people off. That's probably when he ended up on Murgalen's radar."

"Nymphs love their animals," Luna said. "And sex."

Rocco raised an eyebrow. "Ah. So THAT'S where that word comes from…"

Desmond ignored them. "Paranormals are forbidden from harming mortals. If they do, there are consequences. Two years ago, Murgalen targeted Dr. Atticus Thurston and brought him into the faerie world. Shortly after, he lost his mind and left his wife and daughter, abandoned his important research, and vanished from his former life."

"Why?" Cyrus asked.

"Fae have their reasons," Desmond said, "and Murgalen knew what she was doing. The Regulators made her pay the price for ruining the doctor's life. We sealed her in the faerie world for two years as punishment. I did it myself, Mr. Grant. We tried to find Thurston to give him mental assistance, but he disappeared. We thought he killed himself. Imagine my surprise when we spotted Thurston in Uptown with a very powerful magical signature around him. Ironically, he wasn't generating the magic, and we couldn't get anywhere near him because of strong wards. Someone has been protecting him. We now know that it was Murgalen."

"Murgalen never mentioned Thurston," Cyrus said.

"Because she's playing a complicated game," Desmond

said. "She told you only what you needed to know. You're the only survivor we've found that we could communicate with."

"It means she likes you," Rocco said, grinning. "Dare I say, she might even be infatuated with you. If you want your ménage à trois, I'm sure Murgalen could make that happen."

"That's a whole lotta woman for him," Luna said.

"What's that supposed to mean?" Cyrus asked.

"You don't strike me as the type that can hold off a nymph's advances," Luna said. "Didn't you get beat up just before we met you?"

The words triggered him. He jumped to his feet. "Leave my love life out of this!"

"No offense, but if you can't win a street fight, it's going to be hard to win against a nymph's advances," Luna said.

"Calm down, Mr. Grant. There are a lot more things to get upset about," Desmond said. "We've got to find the doctor, and we were hoping you could tell us where to start."

Cyrus relaxed a little. "I want to find him too. But can I change my clothes first?"

"We'll take you home," Desmond said. "But first, we'd like you to take us to the spot where he initiated you."

CHAPTER TWENTY-FOUR

THEY WALKED to the nearest bus station from Luna's apartment in Uptown and waited on a street corner for what seemed like ages for the bus to arrive. The buses never ran on time, but they were especially behind tonight, so much that it ate into the time they would have saved. It wasn't exactly convenient to get from Uptown to Logan Square on the L.

"This isn't going to work," Desmond said, walking away. "I don't like having to take the L, but let's go."

Rocco and Luna transformed into ravens and flew above as Desmond and Cyrus walked below.

It was late, the bone quiet, blackened blade of night that reminded Cyrus of lone saxophone solos on street corners, rats scurrying into the shadows, crisscrossing steel of the L stations accentuated by orange-tinted streetlights, distant sirens, and boulevards that stretched for blocks with no traffic. The kind of night where shit happened, even if you didn't go looking for it. But it was quiet. Too quiet.

What time was it? His body clock told him he should've been in bed. The last time he was out this late, he was with Jules; they went to a show at the Aragon Ballroom in Uptown. They'd sat in the dark ballroom nodding their heads to loud-as-hell goth music that he couldn't understand the lyrics to. They'd slipped out of the building, standing under the old-fashioned marquee bulb lights, and they huddled together in the cold, brisk night breeze. Of course, they should've taken a ride share, but he held her close, his head on a figurative swivel as they walked to the bus stop. It was the kind of night where trouble found you.

He wasn't going to be huddling with Desmond, that was for sure. He walked fearlessly through the streets, not even with a side glance at every alley. The guy was like a child of the night, like the city damn near belonged to him.

Luna and Rocco flying above gave Cyrus a feeling of security. Surely if anything happened, they would be able to see it and back them up. God knew Cyrus wasn't going to fight anybody in human form let alone rat form.

"How long have you been doing this?" Cyrus asked at an intersection as they waited for a car to pass.

"Too long," Desmond said. "We paranormals don't really count our years of service."

Cyrus got the feeling Desmond wasn't going to share much else about himself. Yet he couldn't help but ask. "What part of town are you from?"

"South Side. Born and raised."

"I hope you don't mind me asking, but…what are you?"

Desmond stopped mid-stride as they cross the street. "I'm African-American."

He kept walking, leaving Cyrus in the middle of the roadway. Cyrus jogged to catch up.

"You know what I mean," Cyrus said. "Luna and Rocco are shifters, right?"

"Right."

Desmond pointed down the boulevard where the Lawrence L Station ran perpendicular to the street on elevated tracks. The train screeched to a stop, and the faint intercom voice announced the stop.

Desmond quickened his pace, seemingly wanting to halt the conversation. Cyrus wouldn't stop.

"If you're a raven," he said, making a bold guess, "why aren't you flying?"

"I'm not a raven shifter."

They jogged up the stairs to the station, tapped their cards at the turnstile, and crossed onto the platform. They were the only ones there. Desmond folded his arms and waited silently.

"What's your story, then?" Cyrus asked.

"I got bitten by a vampire, so I can only come out at night, Mr. Grant," Desmond said, irritated. "Then, shortly after that, a mad scientist ripped my body apart limb from limb and rebuilt me. If my luck couldn't get any worse, I got murdered by a Greek god and reincarnated by a voodoo priestess to become her zombie. I broke free of her curse and now my life is my own."

Cyrus's jaw dropped. "Really?"

"Not even close, Mr. Grant," Desmond said.

"Wait, so you're not a vampire, or any of those paranormal beings?"

Desmond sighed. "I know you don't know better, but rule number one about paranormals is that you don't ask what they are. Either you're lucky enough not to find out, or you'll have the grave misfortune of learning the hard way. Remember that, please, Mr. Grant."

Cyrus gulped.

"But if you must know, Luna, Rocco, and I are cut from the same cloth," Desmond said.

Orange lights shone in the distance, and the next train slowed to a stop on the platform, an arrow of heat in the nippy night.

Desmond paused as the doors opened. He glanced up and down the platform, then along the train. "Hold on," he said.

But Cyrus hopped onto the car and plopped onto the first empty seat he could find. "You coming or what?" he said.

Desmond hesitated, but he slipped in at the last second before the door slid shut.

"Mr. Grant, you aren't a civilian anymore," Desmond said sternly.

Cyrus shrugged. "You guys have told me that ten thousand times already."

"You don't just go jumping onto trains," Desmond said. "Not this late at night. Not as a paranormal."

Cyrus gestured to the empty car. "There's no one here. Unless there's a ghost?"

"You're half-animal now," Desmond said as the train rumbled away. "You should have used your senses before you hopped on. If you did, we would've still been on that platform. Oh well, Mr. Grant. Welcome to the school of paranormal hard knocks."

Cyrus screwed up his face at Desmond.

"Shift," Desmond said, glancing around quickly. "Count to thirty, and turn back. Tell me what you sense."

Cyrus stood reluctantly. When Desmond made a "hurry up" motion with his hand, Cyrus turned and shrank into his rat form, landing on the dirty train floor. His whiskers sensed dust and particles of old food immediately. The stench of body odor, faintly detectable to his human nose, nearly overwhelmed him.

Desmond towered over him, a pillar of black distorted in his rat's bubble vision.

But then, he sensed a force that he hadn't in his human form. Something in the air, palpable as smoke, swirling in the next car. It sent a shiver down his body, making him arch his back. Though he couldn't see, he oriented himself toward the energy.

Was it... Singing? Several female voices. Singing a song in an unknown language, harmonizing. Yet the song was faint, like a cologne or perfume on its last under note.

He counted. The energy loomed near, and he felt, quite

literally, like a cornered rat as the train accelerated to maximum speed.

He transformed back into his human self, but the feelings of fear and despair remained.

"Well?" Desmond asked.

"I guess I learned my first lesson tonight," Cyrus said, facing the inner train door. "I never asked for this. I didn't wake up one morning and say I wanted to be a shifter."

"No one does," Desmond said. "Stay close to me. We'll get through this."

Cyrus focused on his rat's sense. Though dulled, he found that if he concentrated, he could feel faint traces of the energy.

The inner train door slid open, letting in the sounds of the wheels clunking against the tracks and the jostling chains that linked the cars. A vortex of air rushed through the car, making Cyrus step backward.

Two women stepped into the car.

One was Caucasian and older—probably in her fifties. She wore her hair tied into a bun, with graying strands hanging down over her face. She wore a green poncho with a hood.

The second woman was Asian and in her twenties. She wore a floral zip-up hoodie and black tights.

The pair looked like they could have been a mother and daughter coming home from a late-night movie, and they were stunningly beautiful.

"Think twice before you stay on this car," Desmond said.

The women approached. Desmond stepped in front of Cyrus.

"We wanted to get a good look at him," the older woman said. "We wanted to see if it was really true."

The older woman tilted her head at Cyrus.

"Mind your business," Desmond said. "Nymphs should know that better than anyone."

"He is our business," the younger woman said. "He might as well be one of us."

The women took two steps toward Desmond, but he barked at them to stay back.

The older woman smiled. "Honey, why don't you come over here and talk to us so we can get to know you a little better?"

Cyrus just stared at them, trying not to show how scared he was. He didn't know what they were capable of, but his body reacted to their presence with visceral disgust. He didn't know how two people who were so beautiful could be also so repulsive.

"Here's how this is going to go down," Desmond said. "At the next stop, you two are gonna stand in the corner over there while we leave. If you pursue us, I will rip you both apart. If you let us go, I will forget we ever met, and I won't pursue this matter any further."

In an instant, the older woman's face shifted into a face lined with bark and triangular teeth, eyes swirling pink with rage.

"You cannot deprive us of one who was created by *our* magic!"

"I'm within my rights to do whatever I deem necessary," Desmond said. "You don't want to start something. If you do, the Regulators will finish it. Just like we locked up Murgalen, we'll punish you as well."

"Murgalen is not one of us," the woman said, snarling. "She has done the fae a great disservice by creating this abortion of a shifter."

"Screw you!" Cyrus said.

"Turn him over to us so that we may enslave him," the woman said. "If you do not, we will have no choice but to report you. And you would be risking a lot, captain."

Captain? Desmond did say he was a precinct captain, but the way the nymph said it wasn't complimentary.

The train began to slow. Behind them, the lights of a platform loomed near.

"Just a couple seconds left to take me up on my offer," Desmond said.

"Just a couple seconds left to keep you in suspense," the woman said. Her face returned to normal, as if she hadn't morphed into the face of a giant tree.

Cyrus, Desmond, and the two women stared each other down as the train ground to a halt at Wilson Station, where several bystanders stood waiting on the elevated platform with a red metal roof.

The younger woman put her hand on one of the windows and chanted something. Flower petals bloomed from the glass, shrouding the car from the bystanders' gazes. Then the woman spoke, and her voice echoed through the intercom, almost magnetic and harmonious in a flawless delivery of a conductor's voice.

"Folks, this train is out of service. You'll have to catch the next train. Thanks for your understanding."

The people on the platform threw up their hands in frustration at the announcement. The train doors opened, then closed. No one entered—they listened to the woman.

The train doors snapped shut, distracting Cyrus from his thoughts. The train accelerated again, and the windows remained covered with flowers.

"This is your final warning," Desmond said.

"This is YOUR final warning," the older woman said. "Do you wish to die knowing that your entire life would have been in vain, protecting a half-blood shifter who should have never existed in the first place?"

Silence.

"He's going to cause problems for us all," the woman said. "We'd be doing the Regulators a favor."

"We don't accept favors from nymphs, and especially not fae," Desmond said. "You ought to know us better than that."

The two women looked at each other, shrugged, and went full tree in half a second. Two giant oak trees with gnarled branches flashed into the car. Their feet were tangled roots, their teeth triangular monstrosities, their eyes swirling pink voids, their skin ridged bark with branches that bent into claws.

Cyrus cursed.

"We will not be denied!" the older woman shouted.

The women slid toward them, their roots leaving long scratches on the train floor.

Something fluttered in through the inner train door. A dazzle of black circled the two women and then landed in one of the younger woman's branches.

It gronked and flapped its wings furiously. From the bluish tint, Cyrus knew it was Luna.

The older tree raised a branch at the raven, but Rocco flew in and circled her.

"Hello," Rocco said in his bird voice.

"Bitch," Luna said.

"Hello."

"Bitch."

The trees swiped at each other, trying to rid themselves of the ravens. But Rocco and Luna were too fast, darting through and around the trees' attacks.

Rocco perched on the uppermost branch of the older woman's crown. Something white ran down it.

"Oops," he said.

The two birds landed in front of Cyrus and shifted into their human forms, sitting on one of the benches, Rocco's arm around Luna, who rested her head in the crook of his shoulder.

"Babe, it's like we're at an evil tree festival," Rocco said. "It's so...revolting, yet I can't take my eyes off them."

"Hello, bitches," Luna said, imitating her raven voice. "Want to keep tangoing?"

The trees continued their slow advance, gnashing their teeth.

A roar stopped them cold.

A six-foot-tall, two-legged beast with brown and black squares on its skin stood next to Cyrus. It bared sharp claws and it wrinkled its rectangular snout, which crinkled in rage. Triangular ears overgrown with fur stood at attention. Black eyes glared at the trees with a far gone expression of the soul that had given itself unto rage. A gold chain hung around the beast's neck. It growled with crooked, jagged teeth that dripped steaming, bubbling saliva.

Cyrus had seen this kind of animal before. Was it—a hyena?

Desmond threw his head back and roared again. He took two hard stomps toward the trees. The car shook under his guttural growl.

"Give him to us!" the woman cried.

"Yeah, about that," Rocco said. "I'm not sure what my werehyena buddy here said, but I know him well enough to guess that he probably told you to screw off or you are going to pay. And he would be within his rights. And you would be smart to get the hell off of this car now, or you'll both be tables in about ten seconds."

"What do you want with me?" Cyrus asked. He figured now was a good time as any to ask the nymphs questions.

"Speak when spoken to, mortal," the older woman said.

"Okay, now you're speaking to me," Cyrus said. "Answer my question."

"You are an abomination of nature," the woman said.

"Abortion, abomination. What other big words are you going to call me tonight?" he asked.

Cyrus knew this route. After the Wilson Station, the Red Line stopped at Sheridan. If he could stop a fight from breaking out before the stop, maybe they could get out alive.

"Why don't you blame Murgalen?" Cyrus asked. "I never asked for this. Your beef is with her."

"We are the arbiters of nature," the woman said. "Nature does not harm itself. Murgalen means to forever damage our reputation."

The train began to slow. Cyrus stole covert glance at Rocco and Luna, who nodded slightly. They would only have one chance.

The train slid to a stop. The doors slid open.

Rocco and Luna bolted from their seats, grabbing Cyrus. Luna shielded him with her body. The trees lashed out and one of them struck Luna on the cheek. Desmond slashed the tree branch clean off with his claws and head-butted the tree, knocking it into the wall. Desmond blocked the door as the trees rushed him, but they stopped at the threshold.

Desmond morphed into his human form, and in an instant, he stuck his foot in the gap between the train and the platform, stopping the doors from closing.

Behind them, several passengers stood with their mouths agape.

"You know what to do," Desmond said. "I already have enough to come after you. Do you want to give me another legitimate reason?"

The tree women glanced at the platform passengers in horror. They shifted back into their beautiful human women forms. The younger woman put her palm on the glass of one of the windows and spoke in a conductor's voice.

"You have seen nothing," she said. "This train will leave the station, and you will not remember what you just saw."

The flower petals in the windows melted away as the passengers remained stunned.

Desmond slid his foot out of the doors.

"This isn't over," the older woman said as the doors closed. "We will have the rat's head."

The train rumbled away, leaving Cyrus, Desmond, Rocco, and Luna on the platform staring after it.

Luna winced in pain. Cyrus inspected her and found a superficial cut across her cheek.

"It's fine," she said.

"Cyrus, you just blew another ménage à trois opportunity, bud," Rocco said, smirking.

"I was going to convince them to try you and Luna first," Cyrus said.

Rocco clapped him on the back. "I knew I liked you."

Desmond started toward the exit. "Let's get out of here before they come back."

They walked the streets to the nearest L station, and when they verified that the next train was safe, they climbed on and rode in silence the rest of the trip.

CHAPTER TWENTY-FIVE

NORTH MILWAUKEE AVENUE in front of the Logan's Crossing shops was empty. Aside from a few lone pedestrians who walked quickly on their way to their destination, and a single car here and there, Cyrus, Desmond, Rocco, and Luna were alone.

Remnants of rain still hung in the air, and the sound of distant tires against wet pavement the next street over gave the street a desolate soundtrack.

The place where it started. If only Cyrus could go back in time. He would have told his old self—his old, naïve self—that he should have just gone home and suffered Becca's rage instead of buying that damn hot dog and sitting on the bench. Then he never would have met Dr. Thurston, and he would be passed out on Becca's couch now.

His old self. Old…He wasn't even old! He wished for his old body back again. He wished that he had never been turned into a rat.

"Walk us through what happened," Desmond said.

"So we're not going to talk about what happened on the L?" Cyrus asked.

"Pretty freaky," Rocco said. "I've been attacked by a lot of things. Beautiful, angry tree women is a first."

Cyrus glanced at Luna's cheek. It was still red.

"You sure you're going to be okay?" he asked. "The cut doesn't have any poison, does it?"

"What makes you think that?" Luna asked.

"I figured anything went in the world of the paranormals," Cyrus said, shrugging.

"If she was poisoned, we would know it," Rocco said. "Poison leaves a distinct signature. Sometimes it kills on contact."

"Back to business, Mr. Grant," Desmond said. "Where did Thurston initiate you?"

"I'll tell you as soon as you tell me what happened back there," Cyrus said. "What kind of animal were you?"

"I have the power to transform into a werehyena," Desmond said. "It's my gift. The animal traces back to South Africa, where it had the magical ability to walk like a human and cast magic. I'm descended from a long line of them."

"Hence why you're the precinct captain," Cyrus said.

Cyrus couldn't forget the werehyena's growl, his willingness to act upon its rage, and the sheer musculature on its arms and legs. If he ever pissed Desmond off, it would be a bad day.

Cyrus led them to the metal bench where he had sat to eat his hot dog before the rat brushed against his foot.

Desmond stood in front of the bench and knelt, inspecting the ground.

Cyrus pointed across the street to the Whisker & Claw office—except it wasn't an office anymore. It was a CD and hobby shop with a red neon sign. The place was closed, and the rows of CDs, vinyls, comic book figurines, and movie posters inside were shadowed.

"This CD shop wasn't here," Cyrus said. "It was in office. Almost like an accountant's office. There wasn't much there. A desk, some chairs, and a back room with a window. And a cage."

"Cage?" Desmond asked.

"For the rat," Cyrus said, pausing to think. "Thurston kept his rat in a cage. Actually, it was a dog kennel."

"A kennel for a rat?" Rocco asked. "Wouldn't it be able to escape?"

Cyrus shook his head. "It hid in the corner."

"Now that you've had a chance to reflect on the matter," Desmond said, "does anything feel different?"

Cyrus wandered down the sidewalk. He glanced again at the CD shop, fixated on the red neon sign.

He crossed the street and tried the door. He knew it wouldn't open, but something wasn't right. The Whisker & Claw office had been different. Way different. This building looked new, like all the other new construction on the block. But he remembered that the Whisker & Claw building was made of old masonry that reminded him of the old shops further up the road, the ones that survived before the shops were built.

"I was just there two days ago," he said. "This building wasn't here."

"I hate to be the one to tell you this, but you were gone longer than two days," Luna said. "Cyrus, you've been gone for three months."

The words hit him hard. "Three months? That's not possible."

"Magic is strong," Desmond said. "When you cross into the fae world, time passes by at a faster rate."

"The city can't tear demolish buildings in three months in Chicago," Cyrus said, remembering many of the eyesore abandoned vacant homes around the city. "There's no way they tore down the building I saw and replaced it with this one."

"Then there must have been some sort of glamour,"

Rocco said. "Fae are good at that. Nymphs are especially good at it. They make people see what they want them to see."

"And hear what they want them to hear too, right?" Cyrus asked. "Like at the train station?"

"Bingo," Rocco said, giving Cyrus a thumbs-up. "You're catching on quick, bud."

"The fae likely used glamour to make you see a space that existed, but they didn't want others to see," Desmond said. He glanced up at the building and pursed his lips. "We can't break through glamour. Not without help."

Cyrus sighed. He was staring at a literal and figurative brick wall. Knots tangled up in his stomach at the realization that he had been utterly and hopelessly screwed the moment that rat brushed up against his foot.

The rat. It looked like a wild rat. Yet Thurston treated it like a pet.

Suddenly, he wanted to vomit.

"That rat wasn't a rat," Cyrus said, hardly able to utter the sentence.

"The one he kept as a pet?" Rocco asked.

Cyrus nodded. "If I didn't know any better, that rat was also a shifter."

Even Desmond was shocked.

Luna tilted her head at Cyrus. "The rat we picked up was a shifter?"

"Picked up?" Desmond asked, folding his arms.

"We saw Thurston kill a rat in the alley behind this place," Luna said. "We delivered it to Cyrus, you know, as a cryptic message."

"*Thurston* killed it?" Cyrus asked. "Where?"

"In the alley," Luna said.

Cyrus dashed down the street. Desmond, Rocco, and Luna followed him down the length of the long, rectangular building and around a corner into a dark alley.

Dumpsters lined both sides of the alley. It was eerily quiet.

A lone streetlight flickered in the middle of the alley. Cyrus ran, counting doors as he went.

He stopped at where the door to the CD shop should have been.

Without saying a word, he shifted into a rat and landed on the wet asphalt. He could see almost nothing now, but he could taste the rain on the ground. And then he sniffed a curious smell, like decay, iron, and feces—God, it was strong.

He followed his nose. His whiskers swept the path in front of him, and he wove around the alley until he stopped at a raisin-sized log.

This was a wild rat's. He didn't know why, but he could sense it. It gave off an earthy, musky odor that wasn't unpleasant to his rat nose. Along with the smell came a message that activated in his rat brain.

Good food here. Keep going.

A constellation of urine called him in the distance, glowing ultraviolet in the night, only visible to his rat eyes. He pulled himself out of this rat's food run and followed his nose toward the door of the CD shop, where another scent of feces attracted him.

This log was different. It wasn't earthy and it wasn't musky. It almost smelled like—he rushed to the door threshold where another message burned into his brain and he seized up.

Amy. Jacob.

Two names. His rat brain spoke them again and again.

Amy. Jacob.

The voice said the names painfully and sorrowfully as if it were mourning. The tone stressed Cyrus out and made him paranoid. Yet he forced himself to keep moving. He found another log a few feet away.

I'm going to die. Jesus Christ, I'm going to die.

He was getting messages from…rat poop? He wasn't sure why, but it seemed natural. His rat brain knew what to do with the smells, and even though probably would have been gross in any other context, Cyrus let instinct guide him, let Mother Nature speak to him.

Cyrus kept sniffing, working his way across the asphalt to another log.

His rat voice warned him.

Danger! Danger!

And then he relived the sensation of a memory. Something sharp stabbing his tail and drawing out blood. A rat shrieking in pain. Cyrus shrieked himself and recoiled from the log, every hair on his body standing on end. His entire body shook with fright.

Then he ran in circles, not knowing what to do. He stopped, started, stopped, dashed toward the wall under a dumpster, where he rested against one of the wheels. The sensation of steel against his body gave him comfort, calming him down. He sensed the final log a few steps away. Another message etched into his mind, and his rat brain screamed at him in a rodent, demonic voice.

I am dead. You are dead, Donovan!

The ground shook and Cyrus threw himself against the wheel, panting. Suddenly, he saw Luna's face straining to see him.

"Cyrus?" she asked softly.

He couldn't say anything. He just stood, shivering.

"Come out," she said. She cupped her hands on the ground, motioning for him to come out.

Slowly, he scurried from out of the dumpster, but not into her hands. He shifted back to human form and dropped to his knees.

"What's the matter, Cyrus?" Luna asked. "Are you okay?"

She tried to pat him on the back, but he pushed her away.

"You took the rat," he said.

Luna nodded. "Yeah."

"It was a shifter," Cyrus said. "He was murdered."

"Not murdered," Luna said. "But dying."

The knots in Cyrus's stomach tightened even further.

"You left him on my doorstep," he said.

Luna nodded again slowly.

"You should have told me!" he yelled.

Luna took a step back.

"He was dying!" Cyrus cried. "I threw him in the trash and just let him die!"

Cyrus held his head in his hands. He remembered the dead rats lying on the ground at Murgalen's feet, how they would never see the real world again.

And this rat...he escaped, only to be left for dead in a dumpster!

No—not *in* the dumpster. He had tried to throw it in, but he missed and it fell!

He pushed himself to his feet and ran out of the alley, tears streaming down his cheek.

"Cyrus!" Desmond said. "Wait!"

Desmond, Rocco, and Luna followed him.

Several shadows were waiting for them, standing in the middle of the street. Cyrus slid to a stop.

He knew the feminine shapes instantly.

"Abomination of magic," a female voice said. The old woman and the young woman stepped into the light, accompanied by more women. They flashed into trees baring their horrific, bark-ridden teeth. Ugly, hair roots swirled under them like evil snakes.

"Your life ends now," they said in unison.

Desmond, Rocco, and Luna caught up to Cyrus.

"So you came back for more, eh?" Rocco said. "I guess you want war, then."

The trees slithered toward them. Cyrus sensed an opening. He dashed to the left, down the street.

Rocco called after him, but Cyrus kept running.

He heard the trees slithering after him, roots scratching against asphalt. But a brutal roar stopped them.

Desmond. He had shifted. He was fighting them.

Footsteps shuffling across the sidewalk...Rocco and Luna were joining Desmond.

He spotted a catch basin nearby. It led to the sewers beneath the street.

He shifted into a rat and squeezed through the cold metal grate, plunging himself into darkness.

CHAPTER TWENTY-SIX

Cyrus crawled through rough and gnarled cement and dropped into a stream of sewage. The smell of ungodly trash instantly hit him. To his rat nose, sewers and trash had started to take on their own unique smell. No place he'd visited was the same. The signatures were always different. This sewer smelled fresher—a higher mix of rainwater and traces of laundry detergent merged with the fetid waste and decomposing trash. The freshness must have been from the laundromat on the corner. The water was warm, making the sewer warmer than outside. The heat radiated off the foamy surface.

Leftovers from the previous rainstorm of the day were still flowing to the Chicago River, but this stream was much more manageable.

The tunnel was too small for him to transform into a human. He wouldn't have wanted to transform, even if he could.

He oriented himself in the darkness, guessing that he was directly under North Milwaukee now. Only a few blocks and he'd arrive at the Wicked Cat.

He found a wall and kept in contact with it as he ran through the tunnel. The sounds of the fighting on the street faded away, replaced by the flowing stream, dripping water somewhere nearby, and the whoosh and ring of an occasional car passing over the manholes above.

He ran as fast as he could, blind in this place, stopping every now and again to assess a large shape, usually a giant piece of trash.

He couldn't stop thinking about the rat. The one who almost made it.

Desmond, Rocco, and Luna just wouldn't understand. Cyrus created this mess, and he had to solve it.

He counted manholes as he went, and he knew them from the faint starlight they let dazzle across the sewer floor.

He stopped upon sensing a bulbous black spider with terrifying fangs sitting askew on the brick wall. The spider regarded him and skittered into a crevice between the bricks. His reticence told him that nothing he ran into down here would be friendly to him.

Twelve manholes later, he sensed the odor of trees and leaves. He guessed that it was Logan Square Park, across from the Wicked Cat.

He paused and listened. No sounds except the usual symphony of the city.

He explored, looking for a way up. His whiskers pointed him toward a small circle in the wall barely big enough for him to stick his head in. Water dripped from it.

This must have been a drain pipe connected to a catch basin like the one he had entered the sewers in.

He dug into the wall and pulled himself into the hole. His head went through first, and then his spine and ribs collapsed until they were nearly flat. He pulled himself through the hole easily. God, if he could only do that as a human! He'd be dangerous.

He crawled over a mixture of metal and cement and stopped at a glowing puddle that looked like a nebula. He'd never seen anything like it. Then the smell hit him.

Urine. So strong!

Something screeched on the other end of the puddle.

Six beady eyes glowed in the dark. Cyrus could barely see them, but there was no mistaking it.

Footsteps approached him, and then he saw sharp incisors underneath the eyes.

More screeching.

Cyrus had no time to react before a giant rat tackled him. They fell into the drain.

CHAPTER TWENTY-SEVEN

Cyrus squeezed through the small hole and crashed into the trickling stream of trash and waste.

The other rat was on top of him immediately, teeth bared.

Cyrus whiffed the rat and sensed that it was a female.

He retreated, but she continued advancing, screeching at him.

If only he could speak to her.

"I'm not your enemy!" he wanted to say.

He glanced at the hole from where they had fallen. The other rats hadn't followed him.

The rat backed up to the hole, her back against the opening.

Cyrus didn't want to fight, but he couldn't help the anger rising in his breast.

Nothing was going to stop him from getting back to the Wicked Cat. Nothing!

He shrieked at the rat, taking a step forward.

The other rat hissed.

He could have run, but he was done running. He had to stand his ground.

"Back off," he wanted to say. But only pips came out of his little mouth.

Then the female rat was upon him again, her claws aimed at his face.

Cyrus dashed to the side, narrowly missing her.

He remembered the fight with Zane. He snapped at the rat's rump, but she dashed out of the way just in time.

Cyrus stood in front of the hole now. He could squeeze through, but if he did, his enemy would bite him into a thousand pieces.

He rushed her, but she scurried up the wall. They were both sideways on the wall until Cyrus bit her on the face.

She rolled down into the water but jumped to her feet quickly.

They circled each other again, Cyrus stepping into the water again.

Nothing was going to stop him. Nothing.

"This is your last chance," he wanted to say again. "You don't know what I'm dealing with right now. I'm living a personal hell and I have to make it right."

The rat charged him again, but he found an opening and sank his teeth into the fur around her rump. He tasted warm blood and fur.

The rat cried in pain.

He twisted and pulled until she submitted to him, lying flat on her belly.

He let go, climbed over her body and into the hole.

She shrieked again, this time not in pain, but in horror and sorrow.

She should have left him alone!

He wasn't planning on hurting anybody! The laws of nature could kiss his ass tonight.

His spine flattened as he sucked himself into the hole. The rat continued shrieking.

Cyrus tracked through the narrow pipe until he saw more beady eyes.

If they wanted some, they were going to get it!

He pushed into the darkness further, squeaking at a high pitch as if to say "Back off!"

The eyes retreated.

Cyrus charged again, sending another warning.

But the eyes kept backing away. Eventually, starlight fell upon them, revealing the rats' bodies. They climbed into another hole.

Cyrus walked until he spotted the slats of another catch basin.

The hole the rats escaped into was small but big enough to fit them.

He heard high-pitched squeals and the sound of bodies clambering over each other. A smell overwhelmed his nose… hairless. Rat-like, but not quite.

His rat brain spoke to him.

Young ones.

His stomach dropped again. He climbed into the hole to see for himself what little his rat eyes would show him. Juvenile rats glared back at him—the same beady eyes he'd seen earlier. Behind them, a nest of writhing rat pups. Though he couldn't see them well, he knew them.

That was why the female had been fighting him.

He nearly fell out of the hole and debated returning to her. But her shrieks were more frantic now. She was practically begging him.

For what?

He felt a primal instinct that made him retreat, debating what to do.

His rat brain told him that he could have killed them.

Replaced them.

But he knew it was just his rat brain speaking, teaching him the laws of nature. He came to his senses and jumped between the slats of the catch basin, climbing out into the night.

Sure enough, he was on a sewer grate just outside Logan Square Park. He couldn't see exactly where he was in the park, but he smelled traces of coffee.

His whiskers drew his attention ahead.

Four rats stood on the sidewalk. They all had food in their mouths.

One rat had a pretzel, and it dropped it upon seeing Cyrus.

Males. All of them. Returning to the nest with food.

Cyrus and the rats froze, eyeing each other.

What had he done?

Hating himself, he ran away, into the street.

A tremendous shadow hovered over him. Looking up, he made out the blurry treads of a boot.

He squealed at the top of his lungs. The boot hung midair. The human above it must have seen him, because she let out a cry and skipped over him, shaking the earth beneath Cyrus.

Fear and his feet carried him as his rat brain screamed for him to run.

The sound of a wheel against the asphalt drew his head left.

He sensed the exhaust, the sheer force, and the humming of an automobile engine before he saw it.

He jumped out of the way and landed between the front two tires of a truck as it flew over him.

He crouched and looked around. No other cars. Yet.

His whiskers fanned out ahead of him and he raced across the street, following his nose and the smell of distant coffee grounds in the air.

He hopped over the sidewalk and into safety.

Were the rats still at the catch basin, staring at him? He figured they were, just as confused as he was.

His heart raced at the thought of the mother he had

ripped from her children. He was prepared to kill her if he had to; she would've killed him, and it would've been for a perfectly good reason. What if someone had ripped HIM from his mother when he couldn't fend for himself?

All he had to do was avoid the mother rat and find another way up into the street. That would have been easier. Safer.

He thought of his mom and missed her. He tasted bitterness and wanted to become invisible.

In the secrecy of an alley, he transformed into a human again, on his knees and facing the wet ground.

Uneven pavement dug into his palms. As his vision sharpened, he saw himself in a puddle. He was the same Cyrus, but he knew in his heart that he was different. And he despised it.

The male rats were still watching him.

"I'm sorry," Cyrus said as if they could understand him.

Seconds later, the rats dipped into the catch basin, and he was relieved to not bear the force of their stares. There was so much to learn still—about the mortal world, the new paranormal world that he'd been forced into, and Mother Nature.

He stood and walked out of the alley and onto the street. He spotted the Wicked Cat, slightly obscured by the oak trees' foliage. A wave of relief washed over him at the sounds of people chattering in the bar and the familiar green and black neon glow of the shop's sign.

He had to see Becca.

But there was one thing to do first.

He crossed the street, transformed into a rat again, and ducked into the alley.

Unlike the other alleys he'd been in, Becca's was a clean as you could get for the city of Chicago. The dumpster lids were closed, with a heavy rock on top of them for good measure. A few record crates that had probably once held imported beer bottles were stacked next to the loading bay door.

Cyrus walked to the dumpster he had tried to throw Donovan into.

His heart fluttered at the sight of the rat carcass just beneath, next to one of the legs. The stench of decay was strong but fading. No prey would have dared eaten this cursed carcass. Not even wild ravens. It wasn't natural, just like Cyrus himself.

He smelled droppings. Unlike the ones in the other alley, these were peaceful. Cyrus sniffed and learned of Donovan's demise.

Donovan slept here for days before he died. He died with regret, but also peace, even though mentions of the doctor were woven throughout the messages in his droppings.

There was anger—so much anger—and fear. An entire multitude of a man in just a few memories. It reminded Cyrus just how complicated people were. He wondered who Donovan was and how much he missed out in life by joining Thurston. It made him sad but comforted that Donovan didn't have to suffer anymore.

Cyrus transformed into a human again. He spotted a broom and dust pan next to the back door. He grabbed it, scooped up Donovan, who was mushy and halfway rotted. He opened the lid of the dumpster and tossed him in.

"I'm sorry I can't give you a better burial," he said. Staring at the rat's decomposing body, he said, "I'll stop Thurston. Not just for you, but for all the others. If I don't, I'll see you soon." Then he closed the lid and waited for a moment in silence, out of respect.

He caught his breath, smoothed out his clothes, and walked around the corner and into the Wicked Cat.

CHAPTER TWENTY-EIGHT

THE WICKED CAT hadn't changed in three months. The same bell chimed as Cyrus opened the door. The customers, who were enjoying their beers, glanced up at him, then resumed their conversations. Becca was playing the Grateful Dead on a Bluetooth speaker in the corner of the bar. The bartenders were still slinging drinks like their lives depended on it, mixing cocktails and pouring frothy beer on tap. The smell of Becca's signature pretzels drifted through the air. And Swiss cheese melt with chives and bacon bits.

Cyrus stood in the door, looking across the bar.

One of the bartenders saw him and looked as if she had seen a ghost. She froze, mid-martini. Cyrus waved to her weakly.

Another bartender saw him and nearly dropped the tray of drinks. Cyrus nodded to him.

Then Becca emerged from the swinging doors in the kitchen carrying a plate of pretzels. She didn't see him at first. He waited patiently as she placed the pretzels at a nearby table. She put her hand on her hip and made small talk with a couple who smiled and joked with her. She adjusted her bandanna as she spoke to them, then tugged her tank down self-consciously and dusted off her apron.

Cyrus approached her from behind, a lump in his throat. He didn't know what to say other than to call her name.

She didn't hear him at first over the bar noise, so he spoke again.

"Hey, Bec."

She froze.

"I'm back," he said.

Becca turned around. She too looked as if she had seen a ghost, as if she couldn't believe she was staring at him.

"I'm sorry," he said, a tear forming in his eye.

She pulled him into a tight hug and cried. He cried too as a few patrons clapped.

"So glad to see you, Cyrus!" Cristián said from the kitchen door.

Becca didn't let him go for a long time, crying into his shoulder. Then she kissed him on the cheek, wiped her eyes, and covered her face, sobbing with happiness, all while saying "God, this is such a relief…"

He let her compose herself, a wave of peace washing over him.

"Where have you been?" she asked finally, taking his face into her hands. She studied him. "Are you okay?"

"I'm fine."

Becca waved to Cristián and told him that she'd be a while. He told them he'd take over and keep watch on the bar.

They walked upstairs to Becca's apartment. Cyrus instinctively reached for his keys but realized they were gone, probably lost to time in the faerie world.

In the apartment, he plopped down on the couch. Becca joined him, a concerned look on her face.

"Well?" she asked. "I thought you were dead."

Dead was a half-true understatement.

"I'm not dead. I was in a lot of danger, but thank God I made it back here."

Becca sighed, waiting for him to continue.

"Bec, I'm in a lot of trouble," he said.

"I figured as much," she said. "We can call the police. What happened?"

"The police can't help me," Cyrus said, looking away.

"Like hell they can't," Becca said. "Cyrus, what did you do?"

"I didn't *do*...anything," he said. "I was in the wrong place at the wrong time." He stood and paced the room. "Bec, I'm a rat."

"Drugs?" she asked. "Please don't tell me you were selling drugs. When I told you to get a job, that's not what I meant—"

"No, Bec. I'm a rat."

"Who did you squeal on?"

"No, you don't understand!"

Silence tore through the apartment.

"I got turned into a rat," he said again.

Becca frowned. "Cy, when you disappeared, this is not what I thought you were going to tell me. You can be honest. It's okay. I'll help. Whatever it takes."

Cyrus shook his head.

The only way to prove it was to show her.

At will, he turned into a rat. His bones shrank and curled into a rat spine. The apartment went blurry, and Becca became a giant tower sitting on the couch. The world blinked from color to muted tones strewn with brown. The sweet smell of flowers flooded his nose.

Cyrus stood on his hind legs and squeaked at Becca. Though he could barely see her face, he saw it wrinkle with disgust.

"What...the...actual...f—"

Cyrus squeaked again and gestured as if he were giving a

speech. Before he could say anything else, she collapsed on the couch.

Becca. Hated. Rats.

And Becca was tough. She beat up all of Cyrus's school-yard bullies, no one messed with her, and she had a bully-ish way about her. But when it came to rats, she was terrified.

Cyrus morphed to human form and sat over her, tapping her cheek and saying her name. She was out.

He looked around the apartment to try to find something that could wake her up. He noticed a beautiful bouquet on the dining room table. He grabbed one of the daisies and dragged it back and underneath her nose.

"Bec, you gotta wake up."

He held her hand. Slowly, her eyelids fluttered open, and she looked at Cyrus, dazed and confused. Cyrus stuck the daisy in his back pocket in case he needed it. Knowing Becca's hatred of rats, she might faint again if he didn't choose his words wisely.

"I should've known you would freak out," he said.

"Freak?"

"I just turned into a rat," he said.

"That didn't happen," she said, sitting up.

"Yes, it did."

She held up a hand and silenced him. "No. It. Didn't. This isn't a fantasy world. How did you do that? Was it some trick? This isn't funny, Cyrus."

"It's not funny. And it's the reason I've been gone. I've almost died half a dozen times already, and I haven't even been back in the city for twenty-four hours yet."

Becca crossed her arms. Her eyes were wild with confusion.

"I just don't understand," she said.

He told her everything. About Thurston. The Damen Silos and Murgalen. His ride through the sewers, and the

Regulators. She listened, clearly unable to process what he told her.

"I only thought I was gone for a few hours," Cyrus said. "When I returned, I learned that I was gone for three months. I didn't know. I'm sorry."

He paused. "I'm not sure how just yet, but things are different for me now, Bec. I'm never going to be the same."

"That explains why you smell awful," she said, rising.

She paced around the living room. "I did this to you. This is my fault."

"It's not your fault. I did this to myself."

"No," Becca said. "I twisted your arm and MADE you go find a job. If you hadn't, you wouldn't have met that weird doctor. Oh my God."

"Bec, you didn't do this. I was just in the wrong place and the wrong time, that's all. But now it's on me to fix this."

Becca walked to the kitchen and braced herself on the counter. She took in a deep breath.

"How are you going to fix it?" she asked.

"I don't know," Cyrus said. "But I came to tell you that I might be gone for a while longer."

"I'll go with you," she said.

Cyrus shook his head. "This paranormal world isn't safe. I've only had a taste of it and I don't like what I see. I don't want to put you in danger. I just didn't want you to worry about me anymore."

"Like I'm not going to worry about you even more now?" she asked.

She paced the kitchen. "I need a drink. Come have one with me."

Cyrus thought of Desmond, Rocco, and Luna. They probably needed him. He had abandoned them. He felt a twinge of guilt thinking of them battling the tree nymphs in the middle of the street.

"I've got to go, Bec," Cyrus said. "I'll be back as soon as I can. Kiss Mom for me, will you?"

Becca shook her head. "You're going to have at least one drink with me. Don't even think about saying no."

She motioned for him to come as she opened the apartment door.

Dr. Atticus Thurston was standing in the doorframe with a revolver. He rested the barrel on her forehead. Becca put her hands up.

"Scream and you die," he said, snarling.

CHAPTER TWENTY-NINE

Thurston pushed Becca backward and crossed the threshold into the apartment. Cyrus's heart raced as the doctor slid the door shut silently and drew the chain. His Cubs cap was pulled low over his eyes and he wore a black windbreaker that concealed a checkered button-up shirt.

"Leave her alone," Cyrus said.

"Hands up," Thurston said, eyeing him. "Unless you want her to die along with you."

Slowly, Cyrus put his hands up where Thurston could see them.

Thurston motioned Becca to keep moving backward until she stood shoulder-to-shoulder with Cyrus. She was as pale as a bed sheet.

"So this is the guy you were worried about," she whispered.

"You told her?" Thurston asked, his face reddening.

"How did you get in here?" Cyrus asked.

"You broke the law of the paranormal," Thurston said. "You aren't supposed to tell them about the magical world."

"Sounds like you broke a few laws yourself," Cyrus said. "Consider us even."

"It won't matter after a while," Thurston said. "Once you're gone, the supernatural imbalance will have only lasted a few hours."

"What about Zane?" Cyrus asked. "Henry and Jenae?"

"On your knees," Thurston said. "Make this easy on me, kid. You served your purpose."

The doctor pointed to Becca first. She gulped and got on her knees.

"I'll get on my knees when you tell me how you got in," Cyrus said, frowning.

"Cyrus," Becca whispered.

"He's going to kill us anyway, so if I'm going to go out, I'm going to at least get answers."

Thurston stared at him for a moment. Then he puffed and tilted his head toward the bouquet. "I had ears listening for you. I knew you'd come back before the night was over."

The flowers wilted instantly, drooping onto the table. Cyrus's heart sank with them.

Shit. Why hadn't he been more careful? The goddamned flowers were *listening* devices. If he survived this, he'd never look at a flower the same way after this, that was for sure.

"Now that you have your answers, get on your knees," Thurston said. "I've got somewhere very important to be."

When Cyrus didn't obey, he forced the gun at Becca and barked at him to get on his knees. Becca's whimpering made Cyrus drop next to her.

"I'm not done with you, yet, Cyrus," a female voice said.

At first, he thought it was Becca, but she hadn't said anything. Her eyes were focused on Thurston's gun.

Had Thurston heard the voice?

No. He was grinning at Cyrus's prostration.

"Sweet Cyrus," Murgalen's voice said. "Thurston knows not what he does, for he is a fool."

Energy pulsed in his back pocket.

The daisy that he had woken Becca up with. It was in his pocket.

"Only you can hear me, my dear," Murgalen said. "Pretend you can't hear me. Listen very carefully and I'll help you and your sister survive."

Cyrus stared ahead.

"Tell him that you know all about him and me," she said. A twisted delight underscored her voice—an emotion that made him sick to his stomach.

"I…know about you and Murgalen," Cyrus said.

Thurston reddened more. "What did you say?"

"Your love won't die in secret," Murgalen whispered. Her voice hummed in Cyrus's ears like an ASMR soundtrack.

"Your love won't die in secret," Cyrus repeated while listening some more. "I've informed the Regulators about you. Even if you kill me, they'll stop you before you ever reach the threshold of the faerie world."

"You're lying," Thurston said.

"Why would I lie?" Cyrus asked. "I was there and saw it with my own eyes. You conspired to break a faerie out of solitary confinement. Even the faerie world agreed that Murgalen should have been locked up. Your days are numbered, Thurston. So go ahead. Kill me like you did Donovan. You'll follow me to hell shortly after."

"Shut up!" Thurston shouted.

Cyrus stopped, unable to believe what Murgalen just told him.

"My love, speak to me," Thurston said, unzipping his windbreaker and revealing his boutonnière. "Do we have a problem like Cyrus says?"

Silence fell hard on the apartment as he waited for an answer.

"I've given you your opportunity," Murgalen said to Cyrus, her voice trailing. "Let's see if you disappoint me. If you wish you live, destroy the flower on his chest."

"Speak to me!" Thurston cried.

Silence.

For a split second, Thurston lowered his gun and fiddled with the boutonnière. "I need you right now, damn it!"

Cyrus sprang forward and tackled Thurston. They fell to the ground, struggling to get hold of the gun.

Thurston's wiry frame was more powerful than it looked. He forced Cyrus on the floor and climbed on top of him. Cyrus kept the doctor's arms at bay and the gun pointed away from him.

Thurston growled at him and Cyrus looked into the man's eyes—into voids of darkness that had no end.

Zane had been right. There was no saving him. No understanding him. No reasoning with him.

Thurston inched the gun closer to a shooting position. Cyrus reached up and ripped the boutonnière off, tossing it away.

"Aaaaaaaaagh!" Thurston cried. He pushed Cyrus aside to grab the flower but—

SMASH!

Becca cracked the flower vase over Thurston's head, knocking him over. Shards of glass rained down on Cyrus and he closed his eyes.

Thurston screamed and staggered back.

But Becca wasn't done—she clocked him with a right hook, knocking the gun from his hand. Thurston grabbed her with his bloody hands and jammed her into a bookcase, knocking books off in a flurry. Becca kicked him in the crotch.

Cyrus followed with a punch to the back of Thurston's head, but his punch was weak. Thurston threw Becca on the floor and grabbed his gun, pointing it at them.

"Shift," Thurston growled, pointing the gun at Becca.

Cyrus's face hardened. Becca crawled backward.

"Shift!" Thurston cried again, firing the gun.

"No!" Cyrus cried.

A bullet struck the ground next to Becca. She screamed, but when the noise dissipated, she was unharmed. It was a deliberate miss.

"Last warning," the doctor said.

"Or what?" Cyrus asked, holding up the boutonnière. He began to crumple it in his hands.

"No!" Thurston cried.

"Shoot at my sister again and you'll fucking regret it," Cyrus said, backing toward the kitchen. He slid open a drawer and produced a lighter. He flicked it a few times, generating a flame. He held the boutonnière over it. "We're both playing for keeps."

"Well, what'll we do, Mr. Grant?" Thurston asked.

"Let Becca go," Cyrus said. "You and I will settle this somewhere else."

"I have a better idea," Thurston said. With his free hand, he pulled out a sea-green ball the size of a pea from his pocket. "Shift into a rat and eat this."

Cyrus knew the ball. Hadn't he seen the same balls in a bucket on the back of Fontanelli's van?

Rat poison.

"Not here," Cyrus said.

"Yes, here," the doctor said.

Cyrus stalked toward the triple bay window and opened one of them. He held the boutonnière and lighter out.

"We leave," Cyrus said. "Or you'll be sorry."

"Hmph," Thurston said. "You've got guts. But I'm not leaving."

Cyrus and Thurston stared each other down.

"Becca," Cyrus said.

His sister walked over to him slowly, and he gave her the lighter and boutonnière. They shared a look of understanding. If the doctor did anything, she would burn it.

Cyrus then transformed into a rat. The green ball loomed near.

He either had to eat it and die like Donovan or shifted back into a human and die with Becca. If he died, he knew Becca could fend for herself as long as she had the boutonnière. Thurston couldn't kill her.

Cyrus approached the ball. Its clean, soapy scent overwhelmed him. Poison masquerading as cleanliness. No wonder rats ate this stuff. He glanced at Becca, who was shaking by the window, and then at Thurston, who waited for him to eat the ball.

"Now," Thurston.

He couldn't put Becca in any more danger. She had too much to live for. Maybe it was right that he died over this. What would the life of a rat look like anyway?

Cyrus opened his mouth and scooped the poison into his mouth with his incisors. Then he closed his mouth and swallowed.

"No!" Becca cried.

The poison didn't take effect on him right away. Cyrus knew it would take a while. He felt perfectly normal, as if he still could take on the doctor in a fight.

He shifted back to a human, but halfway through the transformation, his body jerked wildly, and he got stuck for a moment before shrinking back down into a rat.

"What did you do to him?" Becca asked.

A wicked grin twisted onto Thurston's face. He leveled the gun at Becca. "Give me the flower."

Becca remained still.

"Give me the flower," Thurston said again.

Something crashed into the door, nearly knocking it off its hinges, followed by a beastly roar.

Thurston whipped around in surprise.

Something ripped the chain off the wall. The door flew into Thurston.

His gun went off.

Blam. Roar.

Wood smashing into hundreds of pieces. A night breeze spilling into the apartment.

The fluttering of wings. A gronk. The lighter scorching acorns and baby's breath.

"Damn you!" Thurston cried.

Cyrus tried to morph back into a human again amidst the chaos, but his body jammed and forced him back into a rat.

Then the scuffle of shoes on the hardwood floor.

Blam.

The doctor hollering for mercy, flying through the air… body crunching against a wall.

Footsteps racing through the hallway.

A beast panting. A raven gronking. The boutonnière landing in flaming shreds next to Cyrus.

Becca scooped Cyrus into her palms and he squeaked as he saw her blurry face. Behind her, Desmond in werehyena form stood facing the door, claws ready to strike. He stomped on the boutonnière, rendering it to ashes.

"Vomit," Becca said. "Push it out."

Cyrus lost his balance on Becca's palm. He tried to summon his heaving reflex, but he couldn't. He tried to spit out the poison, push it up from the depths of his esophagus, but that muscle memory didn't exist. Could rats not vomit?

He tried to stand. He wobbled, then fell. Becca's concerned face hovered over his before searing fire tore through his body.

CHAPTER THIRTY

BECCA NOW HAD a metric crapton of problems: her brother was a rat, dying on her palm, a giant hyena man had broken into her apartment and was panting like a dog with hot saliva dripping from his mouth, a raven was perched on her television, and her heart was racing so fast, it was a miracle she hadn't fainted yet. Not to mention the dozens of patrons downstairs who were probably wondering what was going on. Before long, her employees who would come looking for her and ask questions.

She tried to ignore the business and focused on Cyrus. "It's going to be okay."

This convulsing brown, hairy mass in her palm was…her brother. And if she didn't do something, he'd die. She should have been freaking out about the fact that she held a rat in her hand, but instead, she was tender with Cyrus, trying to keep her big sister exterior unbroken. She needed to be strong for him.

The hyena man turned back into a human. A black man with a goatee in a black shirt and gold chain. The transformation should have jarred her, but nothing surprised her at this point.

The raven jumped off the television and shifted into a beautiful woman in a pink flannel shirt. She ran to Becca, lowering herself to Cyrus.

"Why can't he shift?" the woman asked. "Cyrus, what happened?"

"We ought to introduce ourselves," the man said. "We're good guys. I'm Desmond and this is Luna. We're fellow shifters, and we were helping Cyrus before he ran away."

"Yeah, before he ran away and left us to die," Luna said, frowning at Cyrus. But Cyrus was too busy convulsing to reply.

Someone knocked at the doorframe. A hot brunette guy in a leather jacket entered. He cradled his arm against his chest. He looked injured.

"It hurts to fly, so I had to catch up," the man said.

"That's my boyfriend, Rocco," Luna said. "Sorry to have to do fast introductions. You must be Cyrus's sister."

Becca nodded slowly.

"Cyrus is in a lot of trouble," Desmond said. "He shouldn't have visited you yet. He broke another law of the paranormals. You aren't supposed to know that we exist."

Becca backed away. She wasn't going to let anything happen to Cyrus.

"Now you're initiated too," Desmond said. "What did Cyrus ingest?"

"Poison," Becca said.

"Probably infused with magic," Luna said. "If we don't do something, he's a goner."

"He's screwing up our night," Rocco said. "I'm going to send him a bill for my arm. After I destroy the tree nymph that did it, that is."

Becca repeated the words *tree nymph*. "What is going on?"

"We need your help," Desmond said. "Thurston got away. Did he say anything about what his plans were?"

"No. I couldn't follow the conversation," Becca said. "Other than that boutonnière was important."

"You severed his link to the faerie world," Desmond said. "Well done."

"Faeries?" Becca asked. "Like Tinkerbell?"

"Girl, it's complicated," Luna said. "But we've got to get Cyrus to a healer."

She didn't know if she could trust these people, but they seemed concerned enough about Cyrus.

Luna took Cyrus gingerly from Becca and put him on the counter. She caressed his hump and Cyrus lay on his side, looking up at the woman. "You should hurry, I didn't get your name—"

"Becca."

"Well, Becca, we need to get moving."

"Just give me a few minutes," Becca said, remembering her patrons downstairs. She primped her bandanna. At the threshold of her apartment, she looked back at the group. They were circled around Cyrus, comforting him.

"You're making our life difficult, but we're not going to abandon you," Rocco said.

The words gave Becca some relief. She stepped into the hallway and composed herself.

The glass to the security door was shattered. She stepped to the shards, into the night briefly, and back into the Wicked Cat, where rock music was playing from the stereo in the corner, patrons were laughing and chattering, and waitresses weaving around tables, balancing trays of liquor.

At the bar, Cristián saw her and came running.

"What's going on up there?" he asked.

"Everything is fine," she said, "but I have to leave. Can I ask you to take over, pay everyone, and lock up for the night?"

"No problem," Cristián said. "But you look pretty rattled. Are you sure everything's okay? Where's Cyrus?"

"I'm sorry, Cristián," she said, "but I can't give you any details. The Wicked Cat is in your capable hands, okay?"

He shrugged and told her he'd do her proud. Then she ran back upstairs to the apartment.

Cyrus was enduring fits of writhing followed by quiet periods of heavy breathing.

Becca pushed Luna and Rocco aside and caressed him.

"Can we put him in your purse?" Luna asked.

Becca rushed to a coat hook in the kitchen and unhooked a leather cross body purse with a broad front pocket. She emptied its contents onto the microwave. Delicately, she placed Cyrus inside and zipped the pocket around him so that it was snug, but his head peeked out. He stared at nothing, dazed. Becca slung the purse over her shoulder.

"What now?" she asked.

"Becca, we have to warn you," Desmond said. "Cyrus should've never involved you in this."

"But he did," Becca said. "And I'll do whatever it takes to help."

"You may see some grisly things," Desmond said.

"Can't be worse than what I just saw, or the pain of missing my brother for three months," Becca said. "I'll deal with it."

"I know a healer not too far from here, in Hermosa," Desmond said. "But he's not going to be happy to see us."

They left the apartment and called a cab.

CHAPTER THIRTY-ONE

THURSTON STEPPED off the train at Ashland station. There was only one man on the platform this late at night—a homeless guy in a raincoat stocking cap sitting on a platform, dejected. The man looked up at Thurston, and the sight of the bloodied doctor snapped him out of a long frown.

"I thought I was having a bad night," the guy said.

Thurston ignored him.

"If they didn't steal your cash, I could use a buck or two," the man called after him.

Thurston stalked down the stairs. Every step sent a rush of pain through his back. He stopped on one of the landings and rubbed it. That werehyena hurt him something awful when it threw him into the wall.

He needed relief. He imagined all the salves and poultices that probably existed in the faerie world that would take his pain away in seconds.

Since he lost contact with Murgalen, unrest bubbled inside him. He needed her voice, the enrapturement of her sweet words in his mind. He had come too far to be denied now.

That damned kid had destroyed his only link to her. He stewed at the thought of Becca burning his boutonnière.

He had hesitated. He should've blown both of their brains out when he had the chance.

Nothing was going to stop him. He made it to the base of the stairs and crossed from the station onto the street, onto the lonely road toward the Damen Silos.

He was so close.

Two long years. From the time he'd bumped into Murgalen outside the Alsatius Building, he knew his life would never be the same. She sacrificed herself for him. She healed his wounds and paid such a price for it.

How many people had he killed to free her? The love of his life was free—free! And yet...Did she love someone else? Cyrus? After all he had done for her?

The kid was lying.

It didn't matter now. All he had to do was reunite with her, and all would be well. All the struggle he had endured, living in the shadows and the seedy underbelly of the city, would be worth it.

A thunderstorm was gathering again over the silos. The sky was pregnant with rain. The perfect atmosphere for a reunion. The rain would wash away his blood, his pain. Murgalen would emerge from the faerie circle, from the sewers, into his arms. He would embrace her, even if she was in tree form.

He entered the gravel path that led to the gates of the silo.

A horn honked, and a bright headlight blinded him.

A car door slammed.

"Stop right there," a voice said.

Thurston put his hand in front of his face and made out the silhouette of the security guard.

"Can't you read the sign?" the man said. "This is private property. Leave. Now!"

"Oak and ash, rose and thorns, you will let me pass," Thurston said, reciting the nymph enchantment from memory. "I will pass and you will go on with your night."

"Huh?" the guard asked.

Suddenly, Thurston missed the boutonnière pulsing against his chest. It had been the source of his power.

"Leave me alone," Thurston said. "I have business here."

"I'm calling the cops," the security guard said. "Unless you want to be arrested, I suggest you leave."

In a flash, Thurston drew his gun and fired. The security guard dropped into the gravel. Thurston stood over the man and fired several more times until he stopped moving.

He opened the truck and climbed inside. He switched the gear to accelerate and plowed through the gate, ripping it open. The locks broke and the fence posts slanted downward.

He climbed out of the truck while it was still running and spit into the gravel. Then he walked toward the basement, calling Murgalen's name over and over.

CHAPTER THIRTY-TWO

THE HERMOSA NEIGHBORHOOD was just west of Logan Square. They could have walked, but on the cab ride, Desmond told her that they had their fair share of excitement for the night. In the backseat, Rocco nursed his hurt arm. It didn't seem to be broken, but Rocco was in a lot of pain. Luna switched her attention between his arm and Cyrus, who was peeking his head out of Becca's purse.

Becca didn't understand. Why did these people care about Cyrus so much? They were complete strangers.

The cab pulled down a wide boulevard of homes. If Logan Square was the place for hipsters, then Hermosa was the place for families. Logan Square had streets and streets of shops, apartments, and gentrified lofts. Hermosa was a neighborhood of houses: one-and-a-half bungalows with dormer windows, postage-stamp lawns, and wrought-iron gates that blocked entry into the yards. These days, mostly Latino and black families lived here.

Becca had spent a lot of time in Hermosa. When she was getting the Wicked Cat off the ground, she'd rented an apartment here. She signed a six-month lease for a dumpy room in an old lady's basement.

Cyrus's ex-girlfriend Jules lived in Hermosa too.

She thought about Jules. Oh, Jules… She didn't know it, but she was the reason all of this happened. It most definitely was *not* her fault. That honor belonged to Cyrus's eggheaded behavior. But Jules could've let him down gentler. She had been slipping away from Cyrus for a while, but he couldn't see it. Becca never really had the heart to tell him.

Now her little brother was dying from rat poison in her purse. How things deteriorate...

They got out of the cab in front of a mustard yellow house. It was quite possibly the tackiest house Becca had ever seen in Hermosa. The siding was old and falling apart, several black cats wandered the front yard, and the dormer window on the top floor was covered with the 2016 Cubs World Series W white flag, the kind that you saw all over the city after the team finally broke the World Series curse. A neon sign in the front window flashed the word "Curandero" in Spanish.

"Where the hell are we?" Becca asked.

"Becca, just trust me on this," Desmond said as he opened the front gate. Becca sighed as they walked up the front steps to the covered porch.

Rocco pulled her aside.

"Let Desmond do the talking," he said. "I don't mean that to be offensive. But fair warning that the guy we're about to see is a little weird."

"No," Becca said sarcastically. "I figured this would be a completely painless experience."

Rocco shrugged. "Don't say we didn't warn you."

The front steps were in disrepair. Becca stepped over a huge crack.

Loud reggaeton music pulsed from inside the house. A woman rapping in Spanish. The porch windows rattled.

The storm door was covered in wrought-iron gates. Desmond found space between the gates and rapped on the glass.

A few seconds later, an electronic buzz drew Becca's attention to the porch ceiling. A white security camera was watching them.

A heavily accented Spanish voice yelled from the other side of the door.

"Go away!"

"Open up, Gilberto," Desmond said.

"It's too late for this shit!" Gilberto said.

"It's an emergency," Desmond said.

"It's always an emergency!"

"Open up, and we can talk about reducing your sentence," Desmond said.

The reggaeton stopped. The door swung open and a middle-aged Latino man in a wife-beater and jean shorts answered. He was slightly overweight and had a can of Pacifico beer in his hand. The pungent aroma of sage emanated from the house.

Instinctively, Becca slid her purse to her back so that the man couldn't see Cyrus.

"You've got my attention now, captain."

He looked at Rocco and Luna, and upon seeing Becca, he shook his head.

"What are you doing bringing a regular human here?" he asked. "Deal's off."

He slammed the door.

Desmond rapped on the door more forcefully this time. "I don't have time for bullshit, Gilberto! Do you want me to tear this door down?"

"Do it, and I won't heal the wounds when I shoot you!"

"How does a six-month reduction in your sentence sound?" Desmond asked.

Silence.

The door opened again, and Gilberto smiled fakely at Becca. "Lady, you have no idea what you're getting yourself into, but it's an absolute pleasure to meet you." He extended a hand, but Becca just stared at him.

"We might as well all get to know each other, you know?" he asked, glancing at Rocco.

Rocco ignored him.

Gilberto patted Desmond on the shoulder. "Desmond, Desmond. You're looking just as hyena-y as ever, amigo. Next time you come and see me, maybe you ought to get straight to the point. What's up?"

Desmond was unfazed by the man's sudden change in behavior. "Let's talk terms now."

"Aren't you going to tell me your name, lady?" Gilberto asked, looking at Becca.

Becca opened her mouth to speak, to tell him to shut up, but Luna covered it with a palm.

"Never give your name to paranormals you don't know," Luna whispered.

"We've got a shifter in distress," Desmond said. "He's been poisoned. I'll cut you loose from your magical ban temporarily so you can heal him."

"Leather boy here injured his arm, it seems," Gilberto said, cocking his head to inspect Rocco's arm. "You want to use a favor on a routine injured arm? I can save you folks some trouble. Just go to Stroger Hospital. They'll fix that arm right up, big guy. Then you'll be able to turn into a cardinal again."

"Raven," Rocco said under his breath.

"Ah, that's right. You're scavengers too. We all have something in common, then. Too bad you never paid the price for your power."

He turned and motioned for them to enter, disappearing into a dark living room.

Rocco entered first, scoping out the place. When he continued walking, Luna followed. Desmond signaled for Becca to enter and he stood on the porch, looking around the street before shutting the door behind him.

The lights in the living room flicked on. An entertainment system with an old-school big screen TV was playing *Die Hard* with Spanish dubs. A stereo with glowing LED strip lights glowed, a song in Spanish on the display screen with a pause button over it. A bundle of sage smoldered on top of the stereo, surrounded by votive candles and a painting of the Virgin Mary in a picture frame. The air was so thick with smoke that Becca coughed. Somewhere inside the house, chickens clucked.

The room had a sagging corduroy couch that had seen better days and had duct tape patches on the cushions, a glass coffee table with gold lines around the edges. The table was covered in newspaper with neat mounds of herbs—Yerba buena, dill, and basil.

Gilberto strong-armed two wooden chairs from the kitchen and placed them in front of the TV.

Luna and Becca sat while Rocco and Desmond stood. Gilberto plopped onto the couch with his beer.

"After hour visits require after hour fees," Gilberto said.

Becca reached into her purse, but Luna stopped her.

"What are your rates?" Luna asked.

Then Gilberto noticed Cyrus.

"*Dios mio*," Gilberto said under his breath. "That your pet, lady?"

He laughed and sipped his beer. "Only *gringos* keep pet rats."

"It's not a pet," Becca said. "It's my brother."

Gilberto choked on his beer. "I can heal a lot of stuff, but I don't heal crazy."

Cyrus squeaked at Gilberto.

"He's a shifter," Desmond said. "He's been poisoned. There was a spell attached that is preventing him from changing back to human form."

"A rat shifter?" Gilberto asked. He leaned in and scrutinized Cyrus. "Bullshit. I don't believe it."

"If you don't believe us, then there's nothing we can say that will change your mind," Becca said. She wanted to punch this guy in the nose. "If you can't help me cure my brother, then I'll find someone else with the balls to do it."

"Hey, hey," Gilberto said. "No need to attack my manhood."

"Will you help us or not?" Becca asked.

"If what you say is true, I never worked on a rat before," Gilberto said. "Could be fun. Who cursed him?"

"We think it was nymph magic," Desmond said.

"Nymphs?" Gilberto asked. "Never worked with that before. Herbs should work, though. Tell me his symptoms."

"Convulsions, writhing, labored breathing, and confusion," Becca said, pulling Cyrus out of the purse. He rested on her palm and lay on his side. "And lethargy."

Gilberto stroked his chin. "Give me one more."

"I just told you all of them," Becca said.

"You gave me five symptoms," Gilberto said. "I can only work with even numbers."

Becca's jaw dropped. "Seriously?" She puffed. "Fine. Nausea, I guess."

Gilberto snapped his fingers. "Got it. Hyena guy, do I have the express permission of the Regulators to perform this service?"

Gilberto said the words as if he were reciting a boring Bible verse.

"Granted," Desmond said.

"Whoo-wee!" Gilberto said. He disappeared into the kitchen.

Becca turned to Desmond. "You have some explaining to do. You said he was a healer."

"What were you expecting?" Desmond asked.

"I don't know, but it wasn't this," Becca said.

"He's the best at what he does," Desmond said. "If it makes you feel any better, he's serving a five-year sentence for necromancy. Raised his mother from the dead to say a proper goodbye."

"That's…sweet," Becca said.

"Agreed," Desmond said, "Until he made his mom rob a credit union for him before returning to the great beyond so he could pay off her medical bills and save his father from bankruptcy. Imagine an embalmed fifty-year-old woman waving a gun around, smelling of formaldehyde and unable to talk because her jaws were wired shut. She made off with two hundred thousand dollars. The sight of her alone put two tellers in a mental institution. If Gilberto can heal death, he can heal Cyrus. Trust us on this one."

Gilberto returned with a mason jar. "Tell rat boy to piss in this."

"You want my brother to piss in a jar?" Becca asked, incredulous.

"I need to see what kind of sorcery we're dealing with. Piss is the medium I work with, unless you want me to use tarot cards."

Becca accepted the vial and showed it to Cyrus. "I have no idea how we're going to do this," she said quietly. "But this is going to get a little awkward."

Everyone turned away as Becca held Cyrus over the vial, guided his rat...member into the glass, and scrunched up her nose as Cyrus filled it with a dribble.

She handed Gilberto the jar and said "I used to change your diapers, but a urine sample is a first, Cy. You owe me."

Gilberto held the jar up to the light and studied the dark yellow liquid, swirled it, and waited for it to find its level. He broke off a chunk of sage from the stereo and dropped it in. He watched as pieces of the herb sank into the urine, dissolving rapidly.

"There's some bad stuff inside of him," Gilberto said. "Sorcery for sure. Never cured a rat before, but it should be a similar process."

He turned on the stereo, filling the room with reggaeton. The bass pounded in Becca's chest.

"I've waited forever to be back in the game!" he cried, chugging the last of his beer.

In the kitchen, Gilberto whistled to the music as he grabbed items from his cabinets—powdered herbs, tonic water, and other things Becca didn't recognize. He danced around the kitchen as the room filled with a lavender glow, occasionally repeating words from the song—the lines that had curse words. Becca knew enough Spanish to know he wasn't singing about kittens.

He dumped the ingredients into a mortar and ground it into a thick, brownish-orange paste. He put it on a wooden tray along with a fresh brown egg from one of his hens, a new mason jar, and a fan of rue and basil that looked like a sharp, green bouquet.

"This is some craftsmanship right here," Gilberto said, setting the tray on the coffee table.

Desmond cut off the stereo. Gilberto flashed him an annoyed look.

"Blocker's back in force," Desmond said. His hands glowed for a moment and then the magic faded from them.

Gilberto lost the spring in his step. A pall overcame him again as he set the mortar on the coffee table.

"First things first," he said. "I can't guarantee that this will solve your problem completely. I want my magic ban removed if it does. If it doesn't, I want my sentence commuted by two to six months for my time today, as discussed."

"Agreed," Desmond said, folding his arms.

Gilberto grinned.

"Second thing," he said, settling on Becca. "I'm happy to do this because Desmond called in a favor, but I don't know *you*, lady. You're gonna owe me a favor too."

"Name it," Becca said.

"I haven't decided yet," Gilberto said. "I reserve the right to choose at a later date. All I can promise is that it won't be illegal. You like that, don't you, Desmond?"

"You better mean it," Desmond said.

Gilberto clasped his hands together. "I've learned the error of my ways, captain. My people depend on me for *curandero* services. That means healer in Spanish in case you didn't know that. I haven't been able to do Jack shit for them thanks to your power blockers. You think I like slinging sage all day? Anybody can do that. I'm losing my credibility, man. I'm ready to get back to the *real* shit. When I return, every paranormal in Chicago's gonna seek me out after fights. My product is going to be premium. I might even heal a few gangbangers from time to time."

Becca still couldn't believe this guy was a healer. She imagined someone saintlier, in robes, going around quoting scripture—not a guy in Hermosa who listened to loud reggaeton and stored enough herbs to start a farm, and who promised to heal gang members.

"I don't like your offer, but fine," Becca said.

"That's not all," Gilberto said. "Your brother also owes me. Big time. Same terms. I might have use for a rat, in more ways than one."

Becca glanced at Desmond.

"No one gets out of poison and curses that easily," Desmond said. "Do the deal. We'll help you down the road if we can."

Becca inhaled. Maybe she could deal with Gilberto, but she didn't like promising her brother's life away.

She shook the healer's hand.

"A real businesswoman," Gilberto said. "I never caught your name, miss."

"You don't need to know," Becca said.

Gilberto wagged his finger. "Smart human. You're catching on. You can teach your brother a few things."

He took the egg and put it on Cyrus's hump, counting to

twenty-two. Then he cracked the egg in the jar and read the yolk, which turned from yellow to black. Becca's eyes widened.

Gilberto quickly screwed the lid on the mason jar.

He pointed to the mortar with orange paste. "Your rat brother has two problems. The first is that he was poisoned. I don't know how rat poison works, but poison is poison. You have to rid the body of it first, then fight the traces left behind with purification. That's easy. He's going to be pretty weak for a while. Oh, and I recommend that he attend mass for at least a month. The church will help him purify the poisoned parts of his spirit. The second problem is worse. He's got a magical block."

"What's that?" Becca asked.

"Someone specifically banned him from shifting," Gilberto said. "The intent is iron-willed too. I can't remove the block. The only way to do that is to confront the person who cast the spell and convince them to change their mind."

"And if we can't sweet-talk them?" Becca asked.

"You have to kill them," Gilberto said, his voice turning cold. "All I can do is ensure that your brother lives until you can speak to the caster."

Becca just wanted Cyrus to be back to his normal self.

Luna put a hand on Becca's shoulder. "Hey, this is good. It's better than it sounds, trust me."

Gilberto picked up the mortar again and shoved it into Becca's hand. He took the fan of basil and rue and shook it around her and Cyrus as if he were performing part of a ceremony.

"Anyway, you can have this paste. Tell your brother to eat as much as he can stomach. Give it some time to kick in and don't overdo it." He walked to the door, opened it, and gestured them out. "Now if you guys wouldn't mind getting out of my sight, I've got herbs to mix, and I already missed half of *Die Hard*. Have a nice night."

CHAPTER THIRTY-THREE

IN THE DARKNESS of the Damen Silos basement, with only the beam from a lone flashlight, Thurston spread away the dirt from the drain cover leading to the sewer.

He used his bare hands, and they were covered in dirt and grime so filthy and smelly, it was beyond description. He dug his fingers into the grooves on the drain cover and pulled it up. The cover gave a gentle clang as it lifted. Thurston tossed it aside and grimaced as his back screamed at him.

The rusty ladder that sheared away from the wall awaited him.

Bracing through the pain, he lowered himself into the opening and bent around the crooked ladder. The rungs were sharp and muddy. They whined under his pressure.

He reached the second-to-last rung, when the ladder separated from the wall further.

He yelled, lost his grip, and crashed into the sewer below. His flashlight hit him on the face and then went dark.

Muddy water rose to his ankles.

He raised his hands to protect his head, but luckily, the ladder hung by a single bolt.

He fished in the muddy water until his fingers seized on

something lumpy and mushy. He let it go. Then he found the flashlight. He twisted it and thanked his stars that it blinked back on. He shone it on the lumpy mass he had felt seconds ago—the carcass of a bloody rat. One of its eyes bulged with bloat. He jumped at the sight of Zane, then kicked the rat aside.

He swept the flashlight down the tunnel. Water dripped far away. The cylindrical tunnel stretched for what looked like miles. No end in sight. The water below reflected on the surface of the bricks.

He waded down the tunnel to the faerie circle. He counted one hundred paces, then shone the light across the walls, looking for the flowers.

He found them as usual, dead and crumbling between the bricks.

He located the perimeter of the circle and stood directly in the middle.

"I'm here," he said.

The circle should have lit up. It should have been a direct link to Murgalen.

"Speak to me," he said.

Thunder rumbled outside, so strong that he could feel it, even down here.

"You can't abandon me!" he shouted.

His voice reverberated throughout the tunnel, wet and lonely.

There was no one in this darkness except him. With no way up, he'd die down here.

The woman he loved…had abandoned him. Her absence tore open a sizzling hole in his heart. Of lovesickness and rage. If he couldn't have her, no one else could!

At least Cyrus would be dying right now, taking his last painful breath when the rat poison finally burned every vein in his body.

Then she'd be without anyone. No one to love her like he had. No one to sacrifice for her.

Would she find some other poor fool? Bump into him on State Street and fake love at first sight? He pitied that future fool!

And then he was jealous of that fool…

He dropped to his knees and cried like a child. His tears blocked out the little light in the tunnel. He cried for her. He cried for the distant memories he'd left behind. His ex-wife. His daughter.

Two years, down this literal goddamned drain.

He grabbed the revolver on his waist. Without hesitating, he pulled it and held it to his head, and cocked it. He tightened his lips as he forced the cold steel against his temple.

"Where are you?" he cried out. "My blood will be on your hands!"

Silence.

He cried again. Desperate, long, howling cries.

"How could you do this to me…"

Thunder rumbled again, and hard rain pattered on the ground above. Just as his finger descended for the trigger, a rushing sound filled the tunnel.

He barely had enough time to turn around before a tidal wave of storm water smashed into him. The gun fell into the depths, and he gasped as the current carried him into the darkness.

CHAPTER THIRTY-FOUR

On Gilberto's porch, Becca held the mortar as Cyrus rested his front paws on the side and licked the brownish-orange paste. She wondered what it tasted like. Cyrus was reluctant to eat it at first, but he was almost done now, cleaning the sides of the mortar.

"Maybe I should have asked him for a favor," Rocco said, rubbing his arm.

"I told you we *should have* stopped at the pharmacy on the way here," Luna said. "You refused. Said you had to protect us. Literally nothing happened in there, babe. You could be wearing a sling right now." She rubbed his arm and clucked her tongue. "Your arm is really bad."

"Forget I said anything," Rocco said, irritated.

Desmond, who was sitting on the edge of the porch, watching the street, hopped down and ordered a rideshare on his phone. "Last chance to go home if you need to," he said. "I can call another shifter to work back up for you."

"Not on your life," Rocco said. "I told you. I'll be fine. I'm in this until it ends for Cyrus."

Everyone stared at him. Even Cyrus stood on his hind legs and tilted his head.

"I didn't mean it like *that*," Rocco said.

The sky growled with thunder. Thick clouds rolled in over the rooftops.

"Looks like it's going to come down hard," Luna said. "Terrible night to fly."

Cyrus lapped up the rest of the paste. Becca set the bowl next to Gilberto's door. "How do you feel?" she asked.

Cyrus sniffed around on the porch. A little more energy than before. She knew they had to give it time, but she couldn't wait until he was a human again so she could take the burden off her shoulders of protecting…a rat.

Becca stood up and stretched. Her eyes burned with fatigue, the kind of feeling that hit her at the bottom of the night, when the last patrons were sleeping on their arms and she had to shake them awake. She just wanted to walk to her apartment, crawl into her bed, and forget about the world until morning.

Something tugged on her pants.

Cyrus.

She scooped him up and brought his face to hers.

"This keeps getting crazier and crazier," she said.

Cyrus groomed his face, and Becca rubbed his back, triggering him to grind his teeth.

"You shouldn't grind your teeth," she said. "Wait. Actually, that's a rat thing, isn't it?"

She put him in her purse, caressing his head, running the back of her hand against his whiskers.

"What's next?" she asked.

"You heard Gilberto," Desmond said. "We have to seek out the one who cast the spell on Cyrus."

"The nymph?" Becca asked. "Why do I suspect that she isn't going to be kind?"

"Because you're right," Desmond said. "We're off to the Damen Silos. Murgalen will be waiting for us. Whatever she's planning is taking shape."

Two headlamps rounded the corner.

They met a blue minivan on the sidewalk.

Becca waited as the others climbed into the van. She and Cyrus looked up at the billowing clouds lit up by the orange streetlights.

"I can't believe you got me into this mess," Becca said.

Cyrus tilted his head at her.

"Okay, okay," Becca said. "I'll resist a snarky comment. But I have a bad feeling about this, Cy. Am I right or am I wrong?"

Cyrus squeaked.

A wet wind blew as Becca's gaze lingered on the clouds.

"I'll take that as a confirmation that I'm right," she said, jumping into the van.

Thurston flew out of the storm water overflow directly beneath the western silos and crashed into the Chicago River.

Sheets of rain poured onto the surface of the river and he struggled to tread at first as he got his bearings. Up was down and down was up as he finally locked his eyesight on the streetlights of a glowing bridge that seemed miles away in the rain.

He turned to the silos. Ominous clouds swirled around the western silos, which had a tall, graffiti-covered rectangular stairwell attached to the side, with a fire escape. The undersides of the clouds were bubbling.

Thunder rolled, and then lightning struck, turning Thurston's world negative for a split second.

Then he saw it—traced into the clouds on top of the silos —the perfect, round crown of a tree. The clouds wore it like a tattoo. Then the night flashed back to normal.

Singing reverberated around the area. The howling wind obscured it so that the volume swelled and drifted away.

Thurston swam as fast as he could to the docks just beneath the silos.

Raindrops fell for a while on the rideshare van's windshield, obscuring the city outside before the burning in Cyrus's veins subsided. The city lights washed over him in different shades of gray.

The moment he ate the paste that Gilberto prepared for him, he felt better. Was it true that the paste would expel the poison? Since he relieved himself on Gilberto's porch, he felt lighter, more like himself.

Rodenticide was no joke. He swore he'd never put himself in that position again unless it was to sacrifice for someone he loved.

Next time he encountered rat poison in the wild, he'd be careful. He'd know the clean, soapy smell that presaged death. He'd remember the way his body convulsed, how he wobbled and the world around him sounded as if he were in a tin can, how he walked—no, swam—through his life as the chemicals slowly worked their way through his little rodent frame.

How many rats weren't as fortunate as him?

He looked up at Becca, who was watching patiently out the window.

He'd dragged her through hell. And she stood by him.

And Desmond, Rocco, and Luna. They were battle-worn. Cyrus couldn't see them so well, but he could sense it. They were all tired, and there was still so much night left.

They'd have to deal with Thurston. And Murgalen. If they were lucky enough to get to her.

Cyrus closed his eyes and rested against the soft lining of Becca's purse. He let Gilberto's magical healing work its way through his body.

When the van stopped and let them out near the Damen

Silos, and it was time to face the final showdown, he'd be ready. And he would die defending everyone in the car if he could.

But for now, he slept.

The fire escape on the silo tower was in disrepair. Thurston got hold of the rickety stairs and pulled himself onto the first landing of the metal fire escape. Parts of it twisted away from the wall, and the stairs—each a set of three metal rods—were missing in places.

The singing was a little louder now that he had made it out of the water.

Thurston climbed the first set of stairs, rain assaulting him. His foot slipped on one of the stairs and he dangled for a moment before regaining his grip.

As he climbed, the words in Murgalen's voice became clearer.

"Cyrus…my hope…"

Thurston gritted his teeth upon hearing that brat's voice.

"No!" he cried. "Stop!"

A dissonant metal whine drew his attention from her voice.

The steps beneath him snapped and the landing broke away from the wall. Thurston screamed and clutched the metal railing tight as he plummeted toward the river.

The landing bent, creaked, and held.

Thurston looked at the river below, rain needling its surface. He shimmied along the dangling landing and grabbed the next steps.

Murgalen sang Cyrus's name again.

As Thurston ascended the stairs, rage blossomed within him.

He hated her.

Gentle song woke Cyrus. He sniffed before opening his eyes. He licked his lips, taking in the smell of a crisp linen air freshener, wild rain, and the scent of coppery blood. Upon sensing the blood, his eyes snapped open.

The team exited the van a few hundred feet away from the gates to the Damen Silos. The driver didn't acknowledge them and sped away.

From Becca's, Desmond's, Rocco's, and Luna's body language, they didn't smell the stench of death yet. But Cyrus knew they would soon encounter someone dead.

They ran, the pouring rain to the gravel path that led up to the gates of the silos, which were blown apart and collapsed on themselves. A lone truck was in the middle of the path, engine running and headlights on.

Then they saw the dead security guard lying in a pool of his own blood. The rain pattered on his body, his eyes still wide in shock.

Cyrus squeaked and Becca let him onto the gravel. He immediately detected Thurston's scent mixed in with the rain —his blood and sweat.

Lightning struck, illuminating the area.

"Over there!" Luna cried, pointing to something beyond Cyrus's field of vision.

"Murgalen is on top of the silos," Desmond said.

Becca grabbed him and put him in her palm. "Don't die on me," she said. "I don't think I could handle it."

He wished he could tell her that everything would be okay.

Desmond bent over and pointed at Cyrus. "We'll get you up there. I have a feeling you'll know what to do when you're in her presence."

Two claws seized Cyrus and Luna carried him upward, into the howling wind and deluge of rain.

Thurston climbed the final rung of the fire escape and onto the tar and gravel roof of the tower. The wind was stronger up here, with nothing to break it.

The roof was empty.

Lightning struck again, and a ragged sheet of rain splashed on him.

"Where are you?" he cried.

"I'm right here," Murgalen said.

He whipped around to behold a woman in a brown gabardine holding a brown umbrella. She had long red hair and a face full of freckles. She looked just the same as he remembered her on that autumn evening downtown two years ago.

Thurston was breathless at the sight of her. How he'd waited so long to see his love in human form again. Yet he hated her! But how could he hate someone so beautiful?

"You betrayed me," Thurston said.

"I did no such thing," she said, smiling.

She opened her arms for an embrace.

"You don't love me anymore," Thurston said.

She motioned for him and her smile grew wider.

"You sang for Cyrus," he said. "You love him now."

"I love you," she said. "It is time for us to be together. My plan is complete, and you made it possible."

She approached him, her leather boots cracking the gravel as she walked.

"You were speaking to him," Thurston said. "In the apartment. I saw the daisy in his pocket."

"Cyrus is special," Murgalen said. "But not in the way you think."

"So you *were* talking to him. You lied!" Thurston cried, tackling her.

They crashed to the ground. Murgalen did not resist him as he wrapped his hands around her throat.

"I sacrificed my life for you!" he said.

"And now you'll sacrifice me," she said blankly. "After all we've been through."

Thurston squeezed her throat, his fingers digging into her warm flesh.

Murgalen stared at him, and he got lost in her green eyes as she began to sing, her voice constricted and frail from his grip on her.

She sang his name.

He squeezed harder. If he could just end this now…He gritted his teeth.

All the while, she kept singing, her voice shrinking and shrinking as the color drained from her face.

He let go and fell off her. Color rushed back into Murgalen's face as he sat on his knees, sobbing.

Murgalen regained her breath, stood, and brushed the gravel off her raincoat.

"Atty, it has been so hard on you," she said, extending a hand. "It'll be just a little while longer now. Don't you want to see what I've been working on?"

"I…couldn't do it," he said, more for himself than for her. "I couldn't do it."

"I know," Murgalen said. "I forgive you."

He glanced up at her. She smiled at him in the pouring rain.

And then, just like that, he hated himself. Still felt the sensation of his fingers around her neck. He stared at his hands and asked how he could do such a thing.

Murgalen pointed her umbrella at the edge of the roof. Vines appeared out of thin air, combining into thick tendrils with flowers sprouting around them, weaving into a pathway that led down to the roof of the silos a hundred feet below. She began walking down the vines.

The silo roof below consisted of twelve tall cylinders and two long, heavily spray-painted corrugated buildings that ran along the top that divided each cylinder in half. The broken windows were aglow with twilight-colored radiance. Spores of light emanated into the air.

Thurston crawled after her, and then pulled himself into a run to catch up. She grabbed his arm and hooked it under hers and patted his hand.

The rain and wind weren't kind to Luna in her ascent up the silos. It blew her backward, and she had to keep wheeling around in circles as she climbed.

The sheer force of the wind made it hard for Cyrus to breathe, and every thunderclap frightened him. High in the sky with no protection, every instance of thunder shook his entire body.

He couldn't see in this rain. Luna might as well have been flying in pitch darkness. But she kept a firm grip on him, working her way up through the sky.

A loud gronk next to them gave Cyrus some comfort. Rocco.

Luna turned and made an angry call to him. He shouldn't have been flying in his condition, not in these kinds of skies. But he called back and fanned away.

Luna flapped, coasting on the wind for a bit before making a sharp turn. She went diagonal.

Cyrus smelled an intense wave of floral energy that reminded him of wet bark and roses.

They were getting closer. To something.

Luna gronked. Cyrus sensed ground approaching underfoot and he arched his feet. She let go of him and he fell several feet, his tail slicing through the air as if it had a mind of its own.

Despite the crazy wind, he landed on his feet on a gravel roof.

He still couldn't see in this rain. The flight up had made him nauseous. He wobbled on his feet as he strained to see in the darkness. But he trusted Luna.

The floral energy was stronger now. He raced across the roof, his nose to the ground. His whiskers detected a trail of vines descending downward.

The air was more complex now—flowers, wet vines. Bark. Human blood. Sweat. Tears? A floral wave that burned like a hundred blossoming roses. Thurston and Murgalen were on the other side of the bridge.

A human hand scooped him up. Luna. She put him in the wet pocket of her flannel shirt.

Rocco appeared next to her.

Luna punched him in the shoulder and he howled with pain.

"That's what you get for coming up here," she said angrily.

"I'm not sitting this one out, babe," Rocco said.

"Fine. It's your funeral," Luna said.

"Might be all of our funerals if we don't act now," Rocco said.

"Touché," she said. "You're still an idiot, though."

Cyrus squeaked at them to shut up.

"Little guy is right," Rocco said.

Luna and Rocco ran down the vine bridge.

"This is one of those times I wish I would have been granted flying powers with my shifting abilities," Desmond said.

He and Becca stood, watching Luna, Rocco, and Cyrus climb ever higher into the sky.

Becca spotted Thurston in the rain, walking on a vine bridge from the exterior stairwell down to the roof of the silos, arm-in-arm with a woman who carried an umbrella. The covered work floor atop the silos glowed orange. What the hell?

"We have to get up there," Desmond said.

"I don't disagree," Becca said. "But how?" she asked.

"I think I saw a stairwell on the other end of the silos," Desmond said.

They ran across an abandoned maze of gravel, weeds, and cracked concrete barriers toward the silos. A decrepit wooden dock ran along the western silos with a drop-off into the Chicago River. Above, a metal fire escape zigzagged upward. Part of it dangled away from the wall.

"You have to be kidding me," Becca said.

"We don't have a choice," Desmond said, eyeing the first few steps of the fire escape, which were well above reach.

Becca imagined climbing on those stairs and falling to her death. Yep. She'd probably slip somewhere between the second and third landings and die of a heart attack before she hit the ground. The things her brother made her do...

"How good is your grip?" Desmond asked.

"Terrible," Becca said.

"I don't hold that against you," Desmond said, smirking. "Tell you what. We'll do this a different way."

Desmond transformed. He grew in height, and his human face evolved into a hyena face with a wrinkled snout and triangular black nose. His razory black mane bristled in the wind and saliva dripped from his mouth. He growled and yipped, motioning for her to come to him.

Even though she'd seen Desmond in werehyena form, he was more terrifying up close and personal.

Desmond turned around and took a knee.

"This is either going to be the greatest piggyback ride of all time or it's going to result in both of us dying untimely deaths," she said, shaking her head.

She hopped onto Desmond's back and looped her arms underneath his, grabbing her wrists as tightly as she could.

In a single leap, Desmond jumped and grabbed the bottom of the fire escape, pulling himself onto the first step. Becca held on tight as he tore up the stairs, the metal steps bending under his weight.

"Both of you, stop!" Rocco cried. "We're with the Regulators. All of this must stop, now!"

Cyrus peeked out from Luna's shirt pocket. With blurred, fish-eyed perception in the dark, he made out the faint outlines of Thurston and Murgalen holding each other, their backs turned.

Luna balanced on the vines as they shifted in the wind.

"Leave us alone!" Thurston said, turning his head around, a snarl in his voice.

"Not on your life," Luna said.

Murgalen didn't turn around.

"There's plenty of space for us all inside," she said. "Nature does not withhold from her own. Especially birds and rats. You may follow us, children."

Thurston gave her an angry look, but she patted his hand and the duo walked into the covered work floor.

The inside of the work floor was a maze of bent and broken steel beams covered in graffiti tags. The room was awash with the smell of old, cold, and wet shards of beer bottles, dusty rebar, and gravel that had blown in from the stairwell.

Bright light swelled against Cyrus's vision. He scurried from Luna's shirt, down her stomach, down her jeans, and onto the ground, which bloomed with floral energy.

He stood on his hind legs and sniffed.

Next to him, his whiskers beamed an image of a lip of cold steel. Cyrus inspected it. It was a giant, open duct in the floor. He didn't want to think about how far down it stretched.

"Children, there's no point for you to posture," Murgalen said, strolling across the floor.

Cyrus pulled Luna's leg. He gestured to her and squeaked. He puffed himself up to a taller height and sucked in his chest as if he were impersonating a human.

"Oh, right," she whispered. "Murgalen! Let Cyrus turn back into a human."

Murgalen turned, a wide, devious smile on her face. "So you've no doubt removed the poison?"

"How did you know that?" Rocco asked.

"I have ears everywhere," Murgalen said. "Very well. You've earned it, Cyrus."

Murgalen waved a hand.

Cyrus imagined transforming into a human, and his body grew bigger and bigger until he was on his knees, panting.

He was human again. At first, he didn't believe his human eyesight, the air surging into his human lungs, his knees on the broken glass. He was weak, as if he had suffered from the worst flu in his life but was on the mend. It was hard to breathe.

Sharp orange brightness filled his vision. He spotted ducts all over the room, probably drop-offs into the silos. Then he saw Thurston, whose face was full of rage.

"Why did you put me through that trouble to poison him, just to—"

"Sometimes plans change," Murgalen said. "Rather, a life's master plan is just one big improvisation. It's up to each of us to hear the song, Atty, and dance."

Thurston opened his mouth, presumably to curse her, but Murgalen's hand had transformed into a long, thin tree branch, and it coiled around his throat. She raised the doctor into the air.

"Everything is a means to an end, Atticus," she said.

A flash of blue nearly blinded Cyrus. Suddenly, all of the

ducts in the floor were ringed with blue circles of light, rotating like holographic runes.

"Nothing in nature lives unless it earns survival," Murgalen said, "or unless we nymphs will it."

"Don't kill him," Cyrus said. "None of this is his fault. He was dead the moment you decided to use him, wasn't he?"

"You catch on quick, Cyrus," Murgalen said, holding Thurston over one of the ducts. Thurston looked down and hollered at the dark void below him.

"What's your end game?" Cyrus asked.

"For too long, I have watched the life drained from this land," Murgalen said. "We've stood by as humans have polluted our rivers and streams, destroyed our trees. My power weakens by the day. I would expect such foolish behaviors from humans, but from paranormals?"

She sneered at Rocco and Luna.

"What have you done to protect your birthright?" she asked.

"I recycle every week, thank you very fucking much," Rocco said.

"You so-called Regulators claim to keep this world in balance between humans and paranormals," Murgalen said. "But when you suck the last drop out of this planet's useful- ness, you'll die in agony with all the other humans."

Her arm lengthened and kept Thurston over the hole. She walked to one of the broken factory windows and gazed out at the distant skyline.

"It's been said by human scholars that rats are a sign of a community in distress," Murgalen said. "A community crying out in hard times. Isn't that such a beautiful metaphor for this city? Atticus's very existence merely sparked an idea that I was willing to incubate: that nothing—nothing—mirrors the depravity of humanity and paranormals more than rats."

She laughed. "A symptom of nature might just also be the antidote."

"You manipulated him for your own selfish desires," Cyrus said. "Just like you did me. He might not have been perfect, but he was innocent. He and I didn't deserve this!"

"That's why I admire you, Cyrus," Murgalen said. "As Atticus would say, you are a statistical anomaly. You have no idea how many of our experiments over the last year have so disappointed me. I can only work with lost souls. They're pliable. But you—you're oh so lost, Cyrus, but I can't pierce broken hearts that are still mending. That girl did a number on you, didn't she?"

Cyrus couldn't say anything. He *wouldn't* say anything. She was just manipulating him.

"I can be benevolent," Murgalen said. "Your existence will serve as proof of that in light of what's to come."

Murgalen squeezed Thurston harder.

"If no one will stand up for nature, then I must," she said. "As a goddess, it's my right to defend my existence, is it not, ravens?"

Luna rubbed the back of her head. "Well, *technically*, you're correct, but you don't have the right to harm and kill innocent people."

"We'll see about that," she said, tilting her head at Cyrus with a devilish grin. "Let's send a message to all these big, bad paranormals, shall we?"

She dropped Thurston. The doctor flailed his hands and caught the lip of the duct just in time.

Cyrus dashed across the floor and reached out for Thurston.

Thurston grabbed Cyrus's hand.

"Don't listen to her anymore," Cyrus said. "You've been under her spell."

Thurston was heavy. His legs dangled into the black void.

"I don't know what will happen to you," Cyrus said. "But I promise I'll speak up for you."

Thurston grimaced as Cyrus tried to pull him up.

"Rocco, a little help!" Cyrus asked.

Rocco ran toward them. He reached for Cyrus but screamed in pain and recoiled backward as his arm popped.

"Goddamn it!" he said.

"Rocco!" Luna cried.

"I'm fine," he said, scrambling for Cyrus.

"Hang on," Cyrus said to the doctor.

"No," Thurston said, letting go. With his other hand, he grabbed Cyrus's shirt and pulled on him with all his weight.

Murgalen laughed as blue light flashed around them.

Together, Cyrus and Thurston tumbled into the duct.

CHAPTER THIRTY-FIVE

BECCA HELD on tight as Desmond broke the last of the remaining windows in one of the work floor panes as he pulled himself through the opening.

He let her off and transformed back into a human.

Becca got a good look around. The room had a bright orange glow. Several holes in the floor were covered by rotating blue circles. She didn't know what the circles were but guessed that the holes went directly into the silos.

She looked around for Cyrus, Rocco, and Luna. They weren't there.

Only a woman in a brown raincoat and an umbrella, watching them with a smile.

"Who the hell are you?" Becca asked.

Upon seeing her, Desmond held out his hands, generating blue energy from them. He threw two blasts at the woman, knocking her across the room and pinning her to the brick wall.

"Murgalen, where is Cyrus?" Desmond asked, stalking toward her.

Murgalen laughed. "Aren't you going to tell me how happy

you are to see me, Desmond?" Murgalen asked. "Or, how I managed to scoot past your magical sentencing?"

"There'll be plenty of time for that later," Desmond said.

Murgalen's eyes settled on Becca.

"You must be Rebecca," she said. "You and Cyrus look uncannily similar. It's like looking at a female version of him."

"Where is he?" Becca asked.

"*Why* is he is the better question," Murgalen said. "It seems your brother has quite the hero complex, doesn't he?"

"You're going to go away for a long time after this," Desmond said. "You deliberately broke a containment that you agreed to, and you are responsible for the deaths of at least hundreds of innocent people. I'm going to recommend that we throw the book at you."

"I know," Murgalen said. "But when this is over, will there be a book to throw?"

She threw her head back and laughed.

Becca slapped Murgalen, leaving a giant red handprint on the nymph's cheek.

"Stop cackling and tell me where my brother is," Becca said.

"You dare slap a goddess!" Murgalen cried, incredulous.

"I don't care who you are," Becca said. "You'll be sorry if anything happens to him."

"You'll pay for your insolence, girl," Murgalen said.

"Answer the question and we'll see," Becca said.

Murgalen harrumphed. "Your brother may live, or he may die. But if I were you, I'd start making my way down to low ground," Murgalen said. "That is, if you want to listen."

The floor shook. The walls rattled as the silos began to sway. A shrieking sound carried from the faerie circles.

Becca and Desmond looked at each other in horror as Murgalen laughed again.

CHAPTER THIRTY-SIX

A DAZZLE OF blue blinded Cyrus at first.

He was falling.

Fast.

A twilight sky materialized around him. Sunlit clouds with rays that reminded him of God. Birds singing.

A rolling meadow. Coming at him fast.

He transformed into a rat. As his eyes went colorblind, the twilight world transitioned into a pear-colored hue—the same one he remembered from before.

His tail kicked in immediately, steering its way through the air.

Wham!

He landed on his feet. His claws sank into dirt. Swaying grass rose around him.

He sniffed.

Thurston was in the grass.

He pointed his body in the doctor's direction and morphed into human form.

Thurston was on his knees, facing Cyrus. He was grunting, slamming his fist into the dirt, shouting, "No!"

"You stole her from me!" he said.

"I should have just let you die," Cyrus said. "You clearly didn't listen to a word I said."

Thurston hunched over as his body shrank. His scream dissipated as the grass swallowed him.

Cyrus stalked over to Thurston's location. A brown rat stood in the grass, looking around frantically. Upon seeing him, it shrieked.

Then it turned back into a human form, and Thurston sat panting on the grass.

"It's a bitch, isn't it?" Cyrus asked.

Thurston glared at Cyrus with fury and charged him.

Cyrus jumped aside and Thurston face-planted in the dirt.

Beyond Thurston, Cyrus saw the true landscape: the rolling meadow was just a crumbling island. The twilit grass fell away several yards in the distance, and a wall of bubbling gray smoke rose where land met infinity. Tiny red eyes flashed in the wall before drifting upward. Beyond the rats, the Chicago skyline shimmered in rain before dissolving in the wall.

Cyrus stepped back at the sight. They must have been inside the silos.

Thurston roared in pain as he looked up at the grisly scene.

Thunder rumbled and the sky filled with a thousand shrieks as thick gray smoke covered the real clouds.

The earth began to collapse at the wall of smoke, dirt, and rock falling away like dominoes on a mad quest throughout the landscape—right at Cyrus.

Cyrus took off running.

Thurston ran right next to him and elbowed him, knocking him back.

Cyrus fell into the grass and beheld the collapsing ground quickly approaching. Lightning struck in the gray smoke just beyond the edge of the island, and the shrieks within the wall of smoke grew louder.

Cyrus sprinted through the tall grass, where Thurston had gotten a head start.

A giant oak tree with long, wavering branches lay in the distance. Despite the self-destructing landscape, it was calm and serene in the last remnants of evening twilight.

On the other side of the tree, the earth was collapsing too.

Everything converged at the tree.

Thurston started up the tree. Cyrus jumped on him, pinning him against the bark. Then he turned into a rat and scurried over the doctor's back and onto the bark, racing high into the tree.

Soon, there was a pip behind Cyrus and Thurston was a rat too, chasing him.

Cyrus ran onto a thick tree branch as the ground below caved in to a dimension of smoke and eyes. The smoke was smothering and thick.

He knew the eyes.

They were rat eyes. Their shrieks were ascending from the void, enveloping his rat ears.

Thurston jumped onto the branch.

The two rats faced off.

The sky was still picturesque and muted green on one-half of this world—the color of evening to his rat eyes—and the other half, gray, bleak, blistering smoke, and full of eyes.

Thurston wobbled. He still must have been getting used to being a rat. But the look in his eyes was murderous. He was ready to kill. A high-pitched whistle escaped from his mouth.

Cyrus hissed and let out a high-pitched whistle as well, chattering his teeth. He took a step backward, but the branch began to yield.

There was nowhere else to go.

Only one rat was getting off of this branch alive.

He'd tried to save Thurston, but the doctor refused. There was only one choice now.

Thurston screeched at Cyrus, the hair on the back of his head raising like a buzz saw.

Cyrus screeched back and stood his ground, his hair bristling. He stomped the branch with his hind leg.

Thurston took several steps toward Cyrus, but Cyrus charged quickly, making him retreat.

Cyrus hissed again and charged, nudging Thurston backward. Thurston replied in kind, and they were pushing against each other, nose to nose, eyes staring at each other unblinking.

Neither of them dared look down, where the ground was collapsing rapidly. It was only a matter of time before the tree itself tumbled into the void. But Cyrus couldn't think about that now. All he could think about was winning this fight—this slow, biological fight in which there could only be one winner. One victor, one loser. One alive, one dead.

Thurston pushed, sending Cyrus's back feet into a slide. Cyrus dug in with his claws. With as much energy as he could, he pushed off on his hind legs, knocking Thurston back a few steps.

Thurston screeched in anger. Cyrus put his head close to the ground, clicking his teeth together.

Then, without warning, the doctor was on him in a flash, and both rats rose to their hind legs and grappled with each other.

Cyrus remembered his fight with Zane and surprised Thurston with a thump to the face, on his left eye. The doctor squealed in anger. Then Cyrus thumped him on the other eye and pushed the doctor back until he landed on all fours. Cyrus remained on his hind legs.

Thurston retreated a pace and Cyrus dropped to his feet and followed. Then they were on their hind legs again, boxing. Cyrus grabbed the doctor's claws, preventing a nasty thump on his face.

But the doctor was heavier. He leaned his weight on Cyrus this time, learning from the last experience. Cyrus fell backward and leapt back on the branch just before Thurston's jaws snapped at the place where Cyrus's front quarters had been.

The branch was getting thinner the more Cyrus retreated. A few more steps back and the branch would yield again and he'd fall to his death.

Cyrus stomped and hissed. Thurston continued his approach, incisors bared.

Cyrus couldn't take another step back. Thurston lunged forward and bit his front leg. Cyrus screeched in pain as the doctor's jaws sliced through his pink flesh. Thurston let go and slashed Cyrus across the face.

Cyrus stumbled back as the branch began to bend.

The doctor's eyes were furious—he was ready to rip into Cyrus's flesh and draw blood. Thurston shifted his weight onto his hindquarters.

He was going to spring—

Cyrus's tail waved behind him, reminding him of its existence. He coiled his tail around the branch and held on tight.

The doctor sprang at him, claws and yellow teeth bared.

Cyrus let himself fall sideways off the branch. His tail snapped as it hugged the branch and air rushed around him. His stomach caught in his throat as he glimpsed the collapsing meadow below upside-down, then the rough texture of the oak's tree trunk, then the pear sky gradiented with smoke, then the upright crown of the tree as he landed back on the branch, back on his feet, facing the opposite direction.

The act sent Thurston flying off the branch faster than his tail could react. He flipped, grasping his claws at the air.

Thurston shrieked at the top of his lungs and plummeted into the crumbling world below. He smacked against several branches and smashed into the dirt several stories below, landing on his neck. He bounced two times and rolled to a stop on his side, his body unmoving. The earth opened up beneath him, and the void of smoke and rat eyes sucked him down like an ice chip through a straw.

Cyrus held on tightly as he waited for the inevitable. The ground around the base of the tree collapsed like so many trapdoors. The roots of the tree poked out into the void and rose upward as the crown of the tree tilted backward.

Up was down and down was up. Cyrus flew down the trunk as fast as he could as the crown slumped into the void. He climbed onto the first root he could find and held on, staring down the gray smoke.

Hundreds of rat incisors chewed up the tree on their way up from the void. Flashes of lightning in the smoke illuminated their eyes.

Cyrus tried to maintain his grip, but the tree was shaking apart now from the force of the rats.

The root he was holding shook him off.

He tumbled, nose-first down to the meet the face of the rats.

Whatever was down there, he could deal with it, even if it was a quick death. Thurston was dead, and that was half of all that mattered.

He trusted Desmond, Rocco, and Luna with the rest.

He closed his eyes, ready for anything.

But two claws grabbed his back and pulled him upward.

Luna.

She gronked as she and Rocco circled each other, up, up, and away from the mouths of the rats and toward a blue rune in the sky.

CHAPTER THIRTY-SEVEN

Becca kept saying prayers to herself as she climbed down the metal fire escape in the pouring rain. This wasn't how she imagined getting down. She had hoped for the piggyback experience again. Behind her, Desmond carried Murgalen down the stairs, handcuffed with magic. The energy beams let off a low-pitched hum. Desmond's growling werehyena form ensured that Murgalen didn't try anything. Her red hair was a tangled mess in the rain, like a killer horror film. She cackled the whole way down.

How long had it been since her brother jumped in that hole? She wasn't sure, but it was longer than she wanted him to be away. The world kept spinning here despite whatever the hell happened in the fae world.

Becca glanced upward at the silo roof. They still had a long way to go and were about two-thirds of the way down the structure, just past the broken landing. The Chicago River was far below. Too far.

"How do you wish to die, Rebecca?" Murgalen asked. Becca hated the way the nymph said her name.

"Of old age," Becca said flippantly.

"That's not one of the choices," Murgalen said. "The

penalties for assaulting a nymph are limitless. Perhaps I could hold your head below water until the second before you drown, then pull you out. Do it until you die of exhaustion."

"You're killing me of exhaustion right now, that's for sure," Becca said.

They climbed down the stairs in silence for a few moments.

"Or perhaps I can strangle you," the nymph said.

Becca slid across a broken gap where a step should have been. "Or perhaps you can keep your thoughts to yourself."

"I really must decide what to do about this," Murgalen said. "I can't let it stand. What will the other nymphs think?"

"They're probably too busy having sex to care," Becca said, working her way down to another landing.

Desmond laughed.

Murgalen growled. "Don't you dare laugh, werehyena. I'm not done with you yet either. Rebecca, you better keep descending, girl, or you may not like what you see."

"Like I said before, you better not hurt my brother," Becca said.

An explosion rocked the silo and Becca grabbed on to the rusty metal railing to keep her balance.

Becca felt as if the entire staircase would break off from the silo and come tumbling down. Even the river below rippled in mad waves that flowed in the opposite direction of the natural current.

The air inflated with shrieks. The deafening noise engulfed her hearing.

The sky, already gray and gloomy and drenched with rain, clouded with even grayer smoke. Lightning struck, and Becca spotted thousands of eyes like red needle-y pinpoints in the sky. She knew the shapes of those eyes—were they…rats? She gasped and almost lost her grip on the railing.

She. Hated. Rats!

Somehow, she stopped herself from hyperventilating and

caught her balance as the smoke converged into a single column that zoomed toward her.

"What the hell—"

"Get down!" Desmond cried in a beastly voice. Becca ducked and shielded her head. Murgalen's cackles grew louder as the column enveloped them with smoke and ear-splitting shrieks.

Becca almost wanted to jump into the river just to be rid of the noise. She shrieked along with the rats.

Then the column was gone, swirling away over the Chicago River, heading for the glittering skyline.

The shrieking faded. Becca uncovered her head. The area grew silent except for the falling rain.

The first warning sign was the silence behind her. Becca turned around to see the nymph in tree form, completely naked and with a spiky crown of branches, clutching Desmond by the throat. Roots flowed beneath her trunk like wild snakes.

Desmond struggled, but Murgalen didn't hesitate. She launched him off the fire escape into the water below. Desmond roared the whole way down.

Becca gulped as Murgalen turned to face her, grinning with horrific triangular tree bark teeth. Her magical handcuffs were gone, chewed away by the rats.

"What are we going to do with the insolent girl who dared to slap a goddess?" Murgalen asked, stalking toward her.

Becca tore down the fire escape.

"Running scared now?" Murgalen asked. "Typical human —only striking when you won't be struck back. Well, you struck above your race, didn't you?"

"You totally deserved to be slapped," Becca called back.

One more landing down, there was a broken window she could climb through—her only hope.

She tripped and fell toward the window faster than she

expected. She jumped up, narrowly missing a swipe from Murgalen's sharp, branchy claws.

Becca climbed into the window and into pure darkness.

Shit.

She couldn't see anything in here. One wrong step and she'd plummet to her death.

She stayed against the wall, slinking in places where the moonlight crisscrossed the shadows. Then she ducked behind a beam as Murgalen tore out what was left of the broken window pane. A few seconds later, the pane splashed into the river below.

Becca paused, trying to control her rapid breathing.

The ground shook as Murgalen pounded into the room.

Becca tried to get a better look around. The slanted night rays only gave her clues. The room looked like the work floor above. It was hard telling what these rooms were used for—there were so many of them, and the place had been abandoned for a long time, so it was impossible to know for sure since it was in such disrepair.

The room grew quiet except for the pouring rain, distant thunder, and shrieks of the rats, and the quiet scratching of roots against the floor.

"I'll forgive you if you swear your life to me," Murgalen said. "I could use a devout servant. What do you say, Rebecca? My servant, Rebecca...it has a beautiful ring to it."

Murgalen's voice was getting closer.

Becca considered her next gamble. If she moved, she risked betraying her location. If she stayed, Murgalen was sure to find her.

She listened for Murgalen again. The scratching grew closer.

She crouched and inched her way into the darkness, hoping that she wouldn't step in a big hole. Then her shoes crunched on broken glass.

Murgalen screeched and rampaged through the room, her frantic footsteps growing louder as she approached.

Becca lunged into a run, hoping she didn't run directly into the nymph. She steered for another window just a few feet away.

Then the ground slipped from underneath her and she was airborne, falling down but reaching for something, anything…

She landed on her feet on hard, cracked cement. She immediately fell onto her back, gazing upward. A cloud of dust drifted up. She coughed.

Murgalen pounced nearby. Becca crawled backward, but something coiled around her waist and dragged her across the floor. She screamed.

"That's the sound I want to hear," Murgalen said, slamming Becca against a wall, pinning her there. The impact knocked all the wind out of her. "I want to hear you cry for your life. Beg me, Rebecca."

Murgalen squeezed until no air could enter Becca's lungs.

Becca opened her mouth to inhale, but only a dry gasp escaped. Something in her chest cracked, and roaring pain ripped like fire across her body.

A rib.

Becca let out a soundless scream.

Murgalen laughed quietly. "Beg me, Rebecca."

Another rib. Becca threw her head back and tears welled in her eyes and streamed down her cheek. Murgalen inched her face near hers, overwhelming Becca with the stench of wet wood and flowers.

A squeal flitted across the room like an arrow in the darkness. Murgalen shrieked murder.

Becca crashed to the ground.

Murgalen's shadow slithered backward and the nymph shrieked again.

"My eye! You fool! You destroyed my eye!"

A hand pulled Becca up, and the pain in her ribs made the tears fall even harder.

Cyrus's voice whispered to her.

"Bec, listen to me very carefully. We have to get out of here."

"No shit," she said, clutching the space where one of her ribs was. She could hardly breathe. She couldn't stop crying.

Somewhere nearby, Murgalen continued screaming.

"I've got your back," Cyrus said. "But you have to do the walking. Just trust me, okay?"

"I can't see anything," Becca said.

"I know," Cyrus said. "But I came in through a safe path. I'll guide you back through it."

Before Becca could reply, Cyrus was gone. Something crawled down her leg and perched on her left shoe.

Murgalen finally stopped screaming.

"That's it, rat. I'll let you watch your sister die. How does that sound?"

Cyrus stomped on Becca's shoe.

She wanted to shoo him off, but he stomped on her shoe again and tugged her laces to the left.

When she didn't move, he stomped and tugged again until she got the message.

Left.

She took several careful steps to the left.

Then he dug his claws into her shoe until she stopped. He climbed off and pulled her shoelace forward. She followed, and he hooked on to her shoe.

Murgalen stalked through the dark, calling Becca's name.

"Come out, dear. Just give me a hint, will you?"

Cyrus tugged her forward faster and Becca stooped ahead, picking up her speed.

Cyrus hopped onto her right shoe and Becca obeyed. The sudden change in direction set fire to her ribs.

Then suddenly, Cyrus scurried off of her. She froze. Where was he? She began to panic.

Something scratched the walls on the opposite side of the room.

Murgalen roared and went stomping toward it, getting further away. She punched a wall, filling the room with the sound of cracking cement.

A few seconds later, Cyrus dashed on to Becca's shoe, tugging it frantically. Becca listened faithfully, going as quickly and silently as she could.

"Aaaaaargh!" Murgalen cried.

Becca sidestepped right and Cyrus corrected her, pulling her shoe back as she teetered on the edge of some ungodly hole that she didn't want to imagine.

In the faint distance, she spotted moonlight. Her heart leapt and she pushed through the pain.

Murgalen's slithering grew closer.

"I see your shadow, girl," the nymph said, snarling.

Becca broke into a run, ignoring Cyrus, but he dug into her shoe hard, controlling her again, hopping to her other shoe, and guiding her to the side, helping her avoid another hole that her foot nearly slipped into.

They worked their way through the dark, completely trusting each other.

The night rays were closer now.

Cyrus gave Becca one final tug forward, pulling hard and fast. She obeyed and broke into a fast run. Cyrus scurried up her body and onto her shoulder.

Murgalen pounded the ground behind her. Becca could smell the nymph's woodsy breath now.

Cyrus jumped from Becca's head just as she broke into the rainy night, onto the gravel grounds of the silos.

Becca turned around just in time to see Murgalen stumble out of the broken doorway, scratching herself. Cyrus was perched on her cheek, digging his claws in.

Jesus, Murgalen had been feet away from snatching them both.

Becca spied a tall shape waiting next to the doorway.

Cyrus leapt from Murgalen's face just as a hairy fist smashed into the nymph's, sending her flying and twisting on her way down to the ground.

Desmond stood over her, growling.

"This isn't over," Murgalen said. "My protest is just beginning."

She blithely dodged another fist from Desmond and zoomed toward the river, but the werehyena was too fast. More magical energy handcuffs were on her bark-ridden hands before she could move again. She stumbled toward the water, reaching for it.

"It's over," Cyrus said. In human form, he stood next to Becca. "You lost."

Cyrus put one of Becca's arms around his neck, and she leaned on him.

Desmond pulled hard on the magical energy, yanking her back.

"You're going to be locked away forever now," Rocco said, dropping next to Becca. A raven gronked and another human dropped next to him. Luna.

"You won't break out of maximum security next time," Luna said. "No way, no how."

"No," Murgalen cried, reaching for the water helplessly.

"What did you do?" Cyrus asked. "What did you release into the world?"

Over the city skyline, the cloud of rats was dispersing over all areas of the city. Lightning flashed wildly as the clouds descended toward the rooftops. The rats let out a final shriek that ripped through the night. Then all went quiet except for the needling rain and thunder moving across the suburbs.

"If I could only see the looks on your faces when you find out what I've done," Murgalen said, digging her hands into the soil. Desmond yanked her arms again, pinning them behind her.

"I refuse to leave this world with a whimper," Murgalen said. "I'll stand up for what I believe in, and your great-grand-children will remember my name."

She shouted at the top of her lungs.

"A pox on humanity! A pox on paranormals! You will die just as you came into this world—naked and afraid. I've made my mark, but will you heed the warning?"

"How about you speak English?" Cyrus said.

"I'll never allow you to steal my dignity," she said, her face hardening.

She grabbed the magical energy beams from Desmond's hand, wrapped them around her trunk underneath her eyes, and squeezed, slicing her tree body in half. Her decapitated body morphed into human form and tumbled like a bag of bones to the ground.

Cyrus and Becca exchanged a horrified look.

Desmond changed into human form and made the magical energy disappear.

"Welp, folks, that's a wrap," he said, wiping his hands.

"She…killed herself?" Becca asked.

"She's gone," Rocco said. "Hell of a way to clock out."

"But why?" Cyrus asked.

"She didn't stand a chance," Desmond said. "Whatever stunt she pulled tonight, it's going to piss paranormals off superbly. She was a dead nymph walking. I suspect she just wanted to live long enough to ensure her artistry took hold." He glanced out across the river, at the city. "And it has."

The rain relented into a quiet drizzle.

The team stood on the grounds of the silos as the last remains of the eye-filled smoke dissipated over the city and the first rays of sunlight formed pinwheels on the eastern horizon.

CHAPTER THIRTY-EIGHT

One Week Later

"Officials are warning of a sudden death blight that has struck mature oak trees across the city."

Cyrus watched the news report on the flat screen TV in the back corner of the Wicked Cat as he drank a tall can of IPA. An African-American reporter stood on a street corner speaking into a field microphone.

"City workers have reported at least one hundred oak trees that have died within the last week," the reporter said. "The unusual part of the story is that there's no explanation as to why it happened. It's as if these perfectly healthy trees simply died with no warning. I'm here with a certified arborist to tell us his thoughts..."

She offered the mic to a middle-aged man in a polo who spoke with a grave tone. "We want the public to know about this. It's as if someone flipped a switch and a bunch of trees died. We need to look out for our oak trees. I hope this will be a wake-up call to the city to take drastic action to protect our city's canopy."

Cyrus muted the channel.

The evening rush had subsided. The last aromas of coffee were giving way to the scents of tequila, rum, and beer on tap. Becca had the night's first round of pretzels in the oven. The front-loading doors of the bar were open, letting in a warm breeze. A few patrons enjoyed beers at metal tables on the patio.

Becca slid into a chair next to him. There was a lull in customers. She winced as she cracked the tab on a can of soda. Cyrus could tell that her broken ribs were still antagonizing her, but she had strapped two ice packs across her ribs under her clothes and was taking a strong dose of painkillers.

"Nymph's revenge," Becca said, eyeing the television. "Good riddance. Too bad about the trees, though. God knows we need more of them, not less."

She chugged the soda and let out a refreshed sound. Then a fearful look crossed her face. She gritted her teeth and closed her eyes.

"Shit, shit, shit—"

Cyrus ran to the bar and grabbed Becca's pillow that she kept nearby in case of a pending crisis. She snatched it and gave it a bear hug as she burped. Then she pouted.

"Ow, ow, ow..."

She closed her eyes hard, then opened them as the pain passed.

"You just don't learn, do you?" Cyrus asked.

"Like brother, like sister," Becca said. "I *had* to drink something."

"I'd crack a joke, but I don't want to make you laugh," Cyrus said.

"Gee, thanks?" Becca asked sarcastically.

They regarded the news report on mute for a few seconds.

"Crazy how we can see things in a new perspective now," she said. "Most people probably won't even think twice about that story. Just like the giant cloud of rats descending over the city before fading away."

Cyrus laughed. "The news tried to write it off as some weather phenomenon," he said. "Ignorance is bliss, I guess."

"Or maybe the news is part of the conspiracy," Becca said, raising an eyebrow. "Speaking of fabricated stories, how did Mom react to yours?"

Cyrus groaned. "She was just glad to see me. Let's put it that way."

After Becca got out of the hospital and things calmed down, he visited his mom. He told her that he had just needed some time to himself. There was no way in hell she believed him, but she embraced him with a kiss and said there'd be more time to talk later. That bought him time to come up with a good excuse for why he disappeared for three months.

"You're going to help me craft a story," Cyrus said.

"No way," Becca said. "I'm not covering for you."

"Then I won't help you with telling her how you broke two ribs," he said.

"I caught a cold and coughed really hard," Becca said. "Happens to people all the time. Besides, I'm the responsible one. She'll believe me no matter what I say."

"Oh, come on, Bec!"

Becca smirked and raised her soda can to him. "What do you think Mom would say if you told her the truth? That you're a rat now?"

"Rat *shifter*," Cyrus corrected.

"Same diff. What do you think she'd say?"

"How about we not find out?" Cyrus asked.

"It's all good," Becca said. "With all the new clientele, we'll be so busy, we won't have to think about it for a while."

The doorbell chime rang and Desmond walked in, followed by several other people who looked around the place cautiously.

Shifters.

Cyrus didn't know what kind, but they had the same energy as Desmond, Rocco, and Luna.

One of Rocco's arms was in a sling, and Luna had her arm hooked underneath his free arm. She smiled wide at Cyrus.

"The usual?" Becca called out.

"Amen," Rocco said as the group pulled up a table around Cyrus.

One of the shifters—a young man—approached Becca. "Are you the one...who..."

Becca stared at him flatly.

"You know," he said, scratching his head. "Did you slap the goddess?"

"You're a legend," Luna said. "Everyone's talking about it."

Becca grinned. "Why, yes, I did slap the hell out of her. In fact, I even created a drink to commemorate it. It's called the Nymph Slapper," she said. "Whipped hazelnut coffee, Bailey's Irish Cream, brown sugar, and a stick of cinnamon. Want one on the house?"

"Totally," the man said.

Becca braced herself on the table as she stood, fighting through the pain. Then she motioned to Cristián, who nodded and started mixing drinks.

Since Becca was exposed to the paranormal world and had no paranormal powers of her own, she had to be careful. Desmond looked out for her.

Apparently, paranormals needed coffee and alcohol too, so Desmond started bringing his contacts to the Wicked Cat. Business was booming.

Desmond arranged that Becca hire new, paranormal employees who would help her keep the place safe, and he installed wards within all the doors to protect the building and occupants.

And just like that, the Wicked Cat became a hub for the

Regulators, though Cyrus wondered if the real reason for the benevolence was so Desmond could keep an eye on him.

"Have you given any thought to my proposition?" Desmond asked, straddling a chair next to Cyrus. "It's a paid gig. Plus, you get to help people."

"We could really use someone like you," Luna said.

Cyrus still couldn't imagine himself as a Regulator, running the streets with Rocco and Luna and protecting innocent people from the influence of evil paranormals. He didn't exactly want to know what went bump in the night, but he was going to find out whether he wanted to or not. Maybe he owed it to the world to use his powers for good. But what need did the world have for a guy who could turn into a rat?

"Are you still thinking about the job?" Becca asked as she brought a tray of drinks to the table.

"The last time I accepted a job, it turned into trouble," Cyrus said jokingly.

"Whether you take the job or not, you're off my couch at the end of the week, buddy," she said, setting drinks on the table. Luna and Rocco chuckled.

"Cold-hearted," Luna said. "She's not playing around!"

"Becca knows the powers of persuasion," Rocco said. "Maybe she's a paranormal and just doesn't know it."

Cyrus wrinkled his lips. "You have yourself a deal," he said, shaking Desmond's hand.

"Thank God for you, Desmond Lovelace," Becca said, winking at him. "*All* of your drinks are on me tonight."

"Welcome to the team," Desmond said. "We're glad to have you, Mr. Grant."

"Any word on that cloud of rats?" Cyrus asked.

"Nothing yet," Desmond said. "It's the damnedest thing, though."

"More like a ticking time bomb," Rocco said. "Just a matter of time until we find out."

"Maybe it was a prank," Luna said. "Nymphs *are* fae at

the end of the day, and fae love pranks. Maybe Murgalen wants to keep us in suspense over nothing."

Rocco pecked her on the cheek. "That's enough business for today, babe."

"Agree!" Luna said cheerily, swiping the remote control off the table. She changed the television channel to a romantic comedy.

That jogged Cyrus's memory of something he needed to do.

He excused himself from the table.

"Leaving so soon?" Luna asked.

"You reminded me of something," Cyrus said.

Luna touched his arm. "Oh, it's that idea you told me about?"

He nodded.

"Good luck," she said.

"Pour your heart out, bud," Rocco said, saluting.

"Something like that," Cyrus said.

He waved to them and jogged upstairs.

The last few days left him with some thinking to do. About how random circumstances led him to this point—turning into a rat shifter, running for his life, scaring his mother and sister sick, putting his sister at death's doorstep, and unleashing a yet unknown hell on the city.

It was his fault.

Well, not really. He didn't bear the burden of guilt. Sometimes, you're in the wrong place at the wrong time. And sometimes, shit happens. Chicago practically invented that slogan.

He opened the window in Becca's living room, ushering in a nice breeze, and transformed into a rat.

He climbed out onto the window sill and dug his claws into a downspout next to the window, pawing up it quickly, up one story to the roof. The green turret directly over Becca's apartment had a nice ledge that was perfect to sit on and think. The magic hour sun rays reflected off the green metal surface.

There was no roof access from the apartment. He probably shouldn't have been up here, but looking over the rooftops and Logan Square Park brought him peace. Plus, he could sit on the spire with his back to the street where no one on the sidewalk could see him.

He took in Logan Square. The waning sunlight against the old masonry buildings and treetops gave the neighborhood such a relaxing energy.

He had snuck a notebook and pen up to the turret. He'd come up here at least four times to write, but somehow the time and energy never felt right. Now it did.

He grabbed the notebook and opened it to a fresh page.

He'd set a deadline of today. If he didn't do this today, he'd never do it. And he had to.

He glanced over the rooftops and wavering trees as the sun began to set. Then he listened to his heart as he pushed pen to paper.

Dear Jules,

I'll keep this short. I apologize for all the trouble I put you through recently. It's no secret that I really, really loved you. I thought you were the one. When you told me that I wasn't the one for you, I didn't know how to take it. It seemed like the entire universe came to a screeching halt and kicked me out. I didn't know how to cope with it.

Sorry I kept coming by your house. I kept thinking about some way to say something to you that might change your mind. Ever since the minute after you left, I've been kicking myself for getting lost in my thoughts and not saying more to you before you shut the door on me. I felt like I should have spoken my feelings more instead of losing myself to anger. I thought maybe I could get a second chance. But the reality is that it was all about me, and not about you.

I should have considered your feelings. But you know me…I get trapped in the theater of my own mind sometimes, like you told me once.

I apologize without qualification for the pain, frustration, anger, and annoyance I caused you. I've got a lot of growing up to do. I'm moving on. I'm letting you go and focusing on my future now.

Anyway, I wish you all the best with your paralegal career. One day, I'm sure I'll be reading about you. I want nothing but love and happiness for you because you're beautiful, fun, and full of light. You deserve to be happy.

Sincerely,

C

God, this was so fucking awkward! He imagined Jules opening her mailbox, pulling out the letter, frowning at the sight of his name on the return address, and then reading the letter with pent-up anger. Maybe it would do some good. Maybe not. But it didn't matter. He was just doing what he should have done a long time ago.

He read the letter again and hated it. He debated tearing it up and rewriting it, but he decided against it. Luna warned him: "No overthinking. No pondering. Just do it."

He folded the letter, stuffed it in an envelope he had tucked into the notebook's cover, transformed into a rat, took the letter in his mouth, and slid down another downspout to an alley, where he transformed back into a human.

He took the letter to the mailbox on the sidewalk outside the Wicked Cat, opened the hatch, and dropped it in.

Holy crap. He did it. He almost couldn't believe it. Dropping this letter off was like closing a chapter in his life.

Now the whole world was waiting for him.

New job…

New apartment (eventually)…

New friends…

And maybe one day, when the time was right, he'd find a woman that would, as Becca joked, appreciate the supreme and amazingly awkward power of his love.

One day.

But for now, it was time for another beer.

He dug his hands into his pockets and walked back into the Wicked Cat.

THE END.

GET BOOK 2

Cyrus's adventures as a rat shifter (and now super awkward, eligible bachelor) continue in *Book 2: Rat City*.

What exactly did Murgalen unleash on the city before she died?

Turn the page to find out, or grab your copy of *Rat City* today at www.michaellaronn.com/ratcity.